Hidden Names
A Forest Glen novel

Bettie Boswell

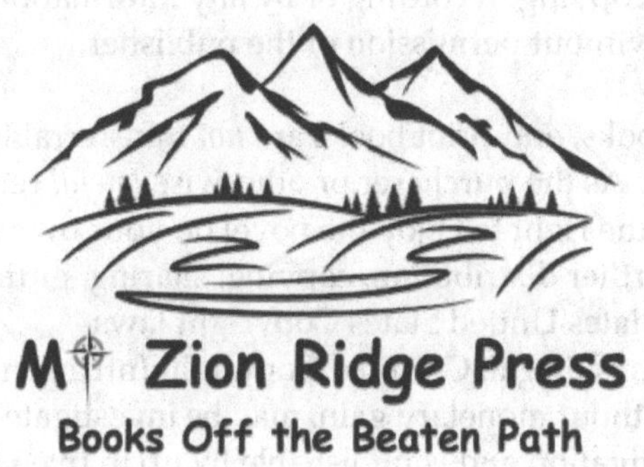

www.MtZionRidgePress.com

Mt Zion Ridge Press LLC
295 Gum Springs Rd, NW
Georgetown, TN 37366

https://www.mtzionridgepress.com

ISBN 13: 978-1-955838-84-p

Published in the United States of America
Publication Date: January 1, 2024

Copyright: © Bettie Boswell 2023

Editor-In-Chief: Michelle Levigne
Executive Editor: Tamera Lynn Kraft

Cover art design by Tamera Lynn Kraft
Cover Art Copyright by Mt Zion Ridge Press LLC © 2023

Chapter One

Amber Whitney walked to the storefront's plate-glass window of her new retail art studio. Clouds darkened the mid-May evening. Streaks of lightning lit up shadowed structures. Across the street a man sat in a large truck, his face illuminated by a cell phone. Maybe he was the artist who made the late appointment. If the man looked for any other merchant, he'd have to wait until morning. Many businesses in the small Ohio suburb known as Forest Glen closed early this time of year. Most of the university students were out of town.

Resigning from being the Forest Glen University's department chair for art, music, and theater, would be worth the change if her plans fell into place. Amber planned on using the time off from teaching at the college to get her business up and running. Suggesting theater professor Scott Hallmark as her replacement had been a wise decision. Since her resignation, the capable man's work ethic assured her the arts leadership was in good hands.

He'd even introduced her to one of the local artists who would have a display in Amber's store. Miss Hope, who owned a fabric store, made quilt-like art from cloth scraps. Her works, displayed in a nearby city's art museum, would surely bring customers looking for the woman's pieces and in the process they'd discover the art studio. Amber worked hard to find quality workmanship for her store. She didn't know if the man coming tonight would meet her standards, but she'd offered to take a look.

Pulling a sweaty bandana from her shoulder-length hair, Amber wiped excess humidity from her cheeks. A wave of satisfaction washed over her as she looked around the room. She'd constructed every shelving unit without help during the last few days. Soon rows of pottery, paintings, statues, Miss Hope's sewn pieces, and other art from fourteen local artisans, including fellow teacher Loretta's paintings, would occupy the space. Samples of her handcrafted jewelry already twinkled from the light-filled glass case near her antique cash register. In a few weeks, her dream of having a market for her artistic jewelry, along with works done by others in her community, would be a reality.

Amber's teaching skills would prove useful through the classes she planned to offer in the back rooms of the studio. Cutting back to part-time at the college would help. She'd already spoken to a future employee about working afternoon hours. Hiring the teacher, who faced reduced hours during the next school year, gave Amber time for covering her remaining college classes. She'd been surprised when Kara contacted her after the school levy failed, but soon learned the teacher was a good friend of Scott's wife, Ginny.

Amber jumped when a gust of wind sent a twig scraping across the plate-glass store window. Clock chimes from the town's courthouse announced the top of the hour. Her appointment should have been here by a quarter 'til nine. She'd give him another fifteen minutes and then head home. Regret about agreeing to the late hour sent a shiver down her spine.

There was room in the store for one more artisan to display their works. The unidentified person who contacted her early this morning, asking for a chance to share his work tonight, might complete her number of anticipated vendors. She'd hoped the man would make it on time, or if he was the guy in the truck that he would come over before the clouds burst wide open. Another rumble of thunder rattled the glass window panes.

A crash erupted from her back door. Lights flickered. Darkness enveloped the room. Crumpled paper scraps from shelving-unit packaging crunched as stealthy steps drew near.

She crouched, ready for an attack. Her dislike for her estranged father led to years of distancing, but not before he had forced her to take multiple self-defense classes. As long as the person creeping her way didn't have a gun, she stood a chance of protecting her store.

"Stop where you are. I will defend myself." There, she had given the person a fair and legal warning.

The footsteps paused. A flash of lightning revealed a figure covered in black, wearing a ski mask, positioned in a similar fighting stance. A pair of open handcuffs glinted from a belted waist, but no weapons were evident on the shadowed intruder.

A rough voice growled, "I'm just looking for some information. If you come easy, there doesn't have to be a fight. If not, I'm taking you anyway."

He slapped her bare arm. It stung. If that was all he had to give, this battle wouldn't last long. She side-stepped, latched on to his fingers, and twisted his hand until she had him pushed against the front window. A flash of lightning revealed a few curls of pale hair sneaking from beneath the ski mask. It also displayed the man from the truck dashing their way. Would there be two assailants?

She pushed the masked man's arm harder. He lifted his leg and kicked her away. The impact sent her rolling. Her right shin screamed in pain as she stood back up, ready to mount a defense against both men. The front door slammed open to the jingle of bells hanging from the handle. Too bad she hadn't locked that entrance earlier.

"Leave the woman alone, or you'll be sorry." The new man's voice broke the two combatants apart. A boom of thunder underscored his words. He stood tall in the doorway. A weapon gleamed from his lowered hand.

"Says who?" the masked man snarled.

"A messenger from MAX." The man's voice commanded respect.

Amber shifted her focus to the taller man and stepped away from her initial attacker. Her father owned MAX Enterprises, or rather, he did before his recent death. The muscular man could be friend or foe. She had no idea.

The masked attacker edged toward her. "The old man's gone. I have higher orders that say she has what my new boss is looking for."

She lifted her hands and moved away from him on slightly bent legs. Her calf bumped the last shelf she'd assembled. A hammer lay somewhere nearby. Her fingers trailed over the shelf and wrapped around the tool as the two men faced off.

"I've got my own orders. Now leave or I'll let the lady finish you off." A click echoed across the dark room as the man from the truck raised his arm and pointed the handgun toward the smaller man. The dark figure relented with a muttered curse and fled toward the back of the shop.

~~~~~

Graham watched the retreating man. He continued to hold his gun in firing position. Movement from the side grabbed his attention as a spinning object flew through the air, knocking the gun from his hand to the ground. *Praise God, the thing didn't fire.*

"Back off, Amber. I'm on your side." His trigger finger stung, but he made no move to retrieve the weapon. He held his arms open and at ease. She'd probably jump him if he bent over. He needed to gain her trust, either as her father's bodyguard or as an undercover federal agent. Graham had orders to protect her and find out what she knew. He had yet to ascertain if she had been part of her father's schemes. Whether she liked it or not, he'd be at her side until he found the information they'd tried to get from her father. The dying man's last words indicated that his daughter needed protection. This morning's email suggested more.

She grabbed his pistol and the hammer she'd thrown through the air. "If you're from my father's company, I don't want your help. All he ever did was bring trouble to Mom and me. You won't find the money he paid for some work I did last year, or my pittance of an inheritance. It's invested in this venue for artists, including myself." She moved behind a low shelf and stepped farther into the shadows.

Graham relaxed his shoulders but kept his arms wide. "I understand you had a complicated relationship with Max Whitney. Unfortunately, he left you a legacy of danger that you're either going to face by yourself or
~~~~~

with the help of someone you can trust."

"I'm not sure you're the person I should trust. Sitting outside my store all night pretending to play on your phone makes me want to doubt you." A sound of disgust rang from the shadows where the woman stood.

She'd seen him and not been fooled. Those instincts might save her life or prove she knew something about her father's business. No one liked to be deceived, especially Graham.

"Look, I worked as your dad's bodyguard since December. His life was in danger and now yours is too. He had something that others didn't want him to share. Earlier today, I received a delayed email from him, set up before his death, indicating that you held the key. The wording indicated he might have sent the message to several people. I decided to stake out your place."

Amber held up a heavy key ring. "I have a bunch of keys. None of them ever belonged to my father. I kept it that way on purpose."

"Obviously your other visitor thought you knew something." He eased his hands down on the shelves that stood between them. "The threat will not go away that easy unless you know something you'd like to share." He studied her shocked face as best he could in the shadowed room and wondered if she knew any details about her father's dealings. "What if I hadn't been watching you from my truck?"

Her stance softened as she placed the hammer onto a lower shelf. She waved the gun toward the back of her shop. "Got a flashlight on your phone? You lead the way down this hallway to my electric box. I need to look someone in the eye before I can trust them."

Graham eased his phone from his pocket between a thumb and one finger. Holding it where she could see, he turned on the flashlight app. As they walked down the hall, which led them to the back of the store, they passed an open office door and two large rooms before arriving at the breaker box. The area didn't show major damage or the presence of the intruder. Light filled the studio shop when Graham flipped the electric box switches back on.

He squinted as his pupils adjusted to the change. Turning to face Amber sent a shock through his system. He studied her green eyes, so like her father's, except for long dark lashes. A smattering of freckles dotted her flushed cheeks. She was even more breathtaking up close than she'd been at the funeral.

He'd seen her from a distance and noted her wavy brown hair but hadn't seen much of her features, other than her bowed head at the wake. Her shoulder-length curls had covered the sides of her face as she'd leaned against an older woman with similar facial features. Both women had seemed more duty-bound than sorrowful at the event. Even though her current body language projected distrust, he felt drawn to the innocent beauty of her unadorned face.

He tamped down his reaction. Innocence had fooled him before. He thought he'd been in love once, only to face betrayal by his fiancée when she dumped him. She had not wanted to accept the dangers of his career. Instead, she'd made other choices and ruined his brother's life too. He forced himself to focus on his current mission. The agency appointed him to watch Amber, and that was all, besides trying to figure out what she knew of Max Whitney's secret.

Did she even know about her father's business? Or did she play a role in what had happened? Trust would have to be a two-way street. Doubt once again seeped into his thoughts. He broke eye contact and brushed past her. Walking to the front of the building he clicked her deadbolt into place. Her gasp, as she raised his gun, made him pause and hold his hands out again.

"I'm just being cautious. Now get that hammer so we can secure your backdoor before any other unwanted visitors arrive."

Graham watched her shoulders slump. She walked to where the hammer sat on a shelf and lifted it with her free hand. He wondered if she might decide to attack again, but then she turned and handed him the tool. Amber's feet tapped behind him as they headed to the rear doorway. The ripped frame revealed her attacker's abrupt entrance.

"Got any nails?"

"Ten." Amber's fingers wiggled in front of his face.

"Seriously?" Graham shook his head. "A few screws will work if you don't have the correct hardware."

Her face sobered.

Graham focused on her left index finger, now pointing toward a shelf filled with tools, screws, and a few finishing nails.

He took what he needed and temporarily pounded the cracked wood together. "You should get a repairman in here to make this more secure. I've nailed the door shut for now. We'll need to leave by using the front. Do you have a security company?"

"They're coming tomorrow. Wish they had come today. A day late and charging more than a dollar short. My inheritance from my father only covered the down payment on this place. I didn't figure I needed security until closer to the studio opening."

Her body relaxed as she hooked one thumb into a belt loop and lowered the gun. He wondered what kind of work she'd done for Max. A wry grin briefly crossed her face. Maybe she thought her alteration of the overused phrase was funny. Graham didn't find any humor in the situation, but he needed to open the lines of communication.

He offered her the hammer using flattened hands. Amber gripped the wooden handle and glared as she handed him his weapon. After clicking the safety on, he returned the gun to his shoulder holster. He followed her into the office and pulled a folding chair in front of her desk.

She sat on the edge of her seat, looking him square in the face. He squirmed, not his best undercover move, but he felt like a kid in school caught pinching his classmate. Her gaze seemed to pierce right through him. He'd hate to be an errant student in one of her art classes who claimed a pet piranha ate his homework.

"Tell me what is really going on, Mister. Don't glaze over anything. My father and I were not close. I figured out long ago that he didn't deserve my complete trust."

Graham rubbed a palm across his chin, stalling for time to think. How much should he tell her? How much did she know? She'd be in more danger if she knew everything, but it seemed that trouble had already found her.

"First of all, my name is Graham Jones." He watched her eyebrows rise.

"Jones? That seems like a good name to use as an alias." Amber's gaze pierced his conscience.

Man, she was good. "Your father knew me as his bodyguard, Graham Jones. That's all you need to know for now."

She crossed her arms and glared. "If you expect me to cooperate, you better know that I expect complete honesty."

He stared at the ceiling, begging for some heavenly help. She was right. It would be better to "let your yea be yea, and your nay be nay." He had always hated the deceitful part of being on undercover assignments. Still, he was under orders. He'd done a thorough background on the woman who sat before him and found nothing worthy of suspicion, other than being her father's daughter. However, he preferred to use caution, based on experience. "I'll share more once you tell me about Max coming to you last November."

She shook her head. "You go first. Tell me your real name and why you're here."

He noticed a tremor in her voice since his mention of her father's visit, but her body language spoke of stubborn resolve. Her father had been an obstinate man. The characteristic ran deep in the family.

"Give me a minute. I have to confirm something." He sent a quick text to his boss while she glared at him. Moments later he received clearance. Graham hoped he wouldn't regret sharing his identity with her.

He looked her in the eye. "Yes, I have a different last name, but it is best you only use Jones for now in case the wrong person hears us talking. You will acknowledge me only as your father's bodyguard in public, regardless of what I tell you in the next few minutes."

He pulled his wallet from the back pocket of his jeans and laid his federal badge out in the open. At least she didn't laugh at his given last name. Her expressive eyebrows did raise a little, but she managed to keep her lips from twisting into a full grimace like a rare, but disastrous blind date once gave him when they shared last names.

"So, what kind of trouble did my father get himself into this time and why am I facing the consequences of his actions?"

Her unhappy expression made him want to reach out to comfort her. Instead, he crossed his arms and leaned back in his chair.

"For years, the government suspected your father made deals with cybercriminals from all over the world. We had no proof and still don't, but we suspect Max was part of a ring and may have been either threatening the others through blackmail or became a danger to them by planning to give their names to authorities.

"When someone attempted to end your father's life during a holiday event, Max made the decision to hire a bodyguard. I applied for the position. We thought my southern background might appeal to him since he had roots in the South. The agency played up the connection. My boss posed as a former satisfied employer and wrote a credible letter of recommendation. After a convincing interview, I worked with Max for the last six months of his life. During my tenure, he hinted about having information that put him in danger. Someone managed to poison him, before he admitted to any wrongdoing. I found a couple clues, but nothing worthy of a court case."

Her face blanched. "You're telling me my father's death was not an accident and I might be next?" Amber wrapped her fingers around a pen and tapped it on the desk. "He attempted to tell me he wanted to make up for the past. I didn't believe him when he came by my campus studio to have some jewelry created. I guess the cheap stones he brought for my use were a shallow excuse to come by and apologize. Too bad I didn't see any transformation. Wish I had. I have no idea what his business did after he dropped Mom and me like a rock during my high school years. I felt no guilt when he offered me a healthy sum of money for making the jewelry. I wish I'd rejected his offer now."

She laid the pen down and leaned against the back of her chair. A remnant of the passing storm rumbled in the background, making her jump. Graham reached for her hand and held it as she trembled, probably in shock. Moments later, both jerked their hands apart at the same time. Her bracelet rattled against the desk.

Graham looked at the jewelry adorning her arm. Stones of various colors twinkled from a silver setting. The piece clunked against the wooden desk where their hands had rested. She mentioned making jewelry for her father. Something seemed familiar about what she had just said. He'd held Max as he passed from what appeared to be a heart attack until the coroner ruled poisoning. Amber's father had muttered words that might have a connection.

"Do you have a Bible?"

"At home, but I use an online one when mine isn't handy." Her expression changed from bewilderment to curiosity. She grabbed her cell off the desk where it had been lying when they first entered the office. "Hmmm, it looks like I have a new message." She clicked on the app, gasped, and pushed her open phone toward Graham.

Give us the information Max Whitney shared or you and those you love will suffer. We'll contact you soon. Be ready.

Graham took a screenshot of the threatening message and sent it to his cell using her device. The number probably came from a burner phone, but it wouldn't hurt to check it out. He would make sure his contacts at the bureau got the threat after he took her to safety. Having her number in his phone also opened up that line of communication, if he gave her phone back.

Her chilled hand brushed his as she attempted to reach for the device. When he turned the cell's power off, and pushed it into his pocket, she lowered her arm without questioning his actions. She was either cool under fire or knew more than she shared.

"Is there anything else you can tell me about your father's visit?"

Chapter Two

"No." Amber glared as she watched Graham step to her side of the desk.

He grabbed her arm and pulled her up to a standing position. She flinched. The place where the creep had slapped her hurt under Graham's grasp. She must be overreacting to the adrenaline still coursing through her veins. There was no way the sissy fighter did that much damage.

"Then grab your gear. We've got to go."

Graham's command sounded like a line from one of the few television shows she watched.

"Uh, you have my gear. Most of the time, I only carry a few things in the wallet attached to the back of my cell phone." She wondered why he'd taken her phone but figured it had something to do with the text message. She did not plan on him keeping it. The device contained her whole life plan.

"Well, get your keys and lock up. We're not staying here tonight." He peered into the hallway and looked both ways before motioning for her to follow. She felt like she'd entered the set of a cheap suspense movie, which made tension radiate through her chest. Whenever troubles happened, she often reacted with humor.

"Of course not, this is an art studio, not a studio apartment." She turned away from his march toward the front door and went back to turn off the lights. Darkness surrounded her, sending a shiver down her spine as she hustled to catch up with her very own special federal agent. If tonight hadn't been so scary, it might have been hilarious to know she could make a Fed squirm when he tried to interrogate her. Teachers had their own brand of special investigative tools, and she knew how to use them. Those powers might come in handy as she tried to figure out the mess her father had put her in.

Locking the front door required a different key than the one she'd used to enter the back entrance where her car sat. She turned after struggling to lock up with the rarely used key and found herself facing Graham's chest.

He swiveled his head from side to side as his arms leaned against the doorframe and surrounded her. Warmth danced across her cheeks as she stood under the near stranger's arms. *Wonder what he'd do if I hugged him. Probably throw me into a choke hold or something.*

"Graham." Her voice came out sounding wimpy. She cleared her throat and tapped his chest. "I need to get my car from the back alley."

"Not tonight. We'll have someone check your vehicle for tracking devices or bombs in the morning. You're not using it before then. We have to get you to a safe place." He took her elbow, hustled her across the street and around the side of his truck.

Once he opened the door to the passenger side, he stood behind her until she'd climbed onto the cab's high seat. While she clicked her seatbelt into place, he slammed the door and walked around to his side. She watched him scan the area as he circled the vehicle.

The engine roared to life immediately after he took his place in the driver's seat. Amber could have sworn she felt some G-forces as they pulled away from the curb. So much for a subtle exit. If there were bad guys watching, they'd be on their tail any minute.

She leaned over to check the side mirrors and only saw rain-slicked pavement. "I hate to mess with your plans, but may I stop by my apartment for a change of clothing and a few necessities? I've been working on the shop all day, as you can probably smell." She flapped her arms and watched a slow grin spread across his handsome face. One hand cupped his nose as he faked a cough.

"Good try, but not a wise move. One of my fellow agents can bring clothing and other supplies to the safe house. I promise you, we can take care of your needs." He slowed the wipers, then turned down a street heading north.

The need to stop at her apartment brought a memory to mind, one she thought Graham would want to know about. "You asked about my father's last visit. He did give me his mother's family Bible, which seemed odd to me. Dad wasn't much for family or Christianity. Maybe he left a clue in the book."

She heard him huff.

"We'll swing by to get the Bible, but make it quick." He tapped a setting on his phone, and a twangy country voice blared directions to her apartment.

"You really are a southern boy." A sense of violation made Amber squirm. He knew where she lived without asking. How many people besides him were watching her home and business?

"Yep."

She sat in silence after his one-word reply. The woman's syrupy voice guided them closer to her apartment with each spoken direction, reminding her of Grandmother Whitney's accent. It had been a long time since she'd visited her granny's grave in Alabama. She'd been surprised Graham had gained favor with her father by using his connection to the region. Her father had done his best to erase all traces of the South from his life. Too bad she couldn't erase what happened earlier at the studio.

Amber pulled down the sun visor and opened its mirror. Her hair was a mess. She pushed fingers through tangled curls while checking for traffic. No headlights appeared in the empty street. Relieved, she continued the conversation.

"I thought I heard a little bit of sweet old Alabama in your voice earlier. You didn't have to work hard to cozy up to Dad."

"Good guess, but Georgia is what I have on my tongue. Though, it's been a while and the accent has faded." He checked his mirrors and swung into the shadowy parking lot beside her apartment. "Is it always this dark here?"

"No, it looks like something happened to the streetlight by my building." His truck's headlights reflected off broken shards of glass lying under the darkened light.

"Hand me your keys. Stick to me like a tick." He held out his hand after shutting off the truck's engine.

She fisted her keys. "My lock is tricky. I'll let you in." Amber jumped down from the truck and waited to see if anyone, other than Graham, growled at her decision to get out on her own. Her keys poked through her fingers like brass knuckles with points, another self-defense lesson from one of the classes her father had provided. She wasn't totally helpless.

Graham stepped near and motioned for her to follow him into the apartment complex. She could tell he knew her apartment location when he headed for her building. That should have made her uncomfortable, but at the moment she welcomed the knowledge and company. Though, she would never admit to him anything about the avalanche of fear coursing through her body.

They edged closer to her unit. She pressed her back against the rough brick wall, then followed him up the stairs to her door, which swung open when Graham tested it.

He shouted, "Federal agent. Is anyone here?" Silence. Whoever had opened the entry had left no marks, and most likely had departed. No sounds came from inside. From the lack of damage to the lock and frame, a professional lock-picking thief had been in her home.

One glance around her apartment and the bottom dropped out of her world like a high-speed roller coaster. It made her sick. So did real-life roller coasters for that matter. She fought nausea as she pushed her way around Graham. He grabbed her shoulders and restrained her from entering. Lamplight filled the living room, revealing sliced couch cushions on the floor and bookshelves in disarray.

Graham took her arm and led her back out to his truck. "I need to call my team and the local cops. You can't go in right now. Is there someone nearby who might have heard the intruders?"

"Not really. Most of my neighbors are students or instructors, and the college is on a break. Mom is several hours from here, but you probably know that, don't you?"

He nodded, then turned away to describe the situation to a 911 operator. Amber fingered the bracelet on her wrist. Other than the inheritance and large payment for the jewelry assignment, she'd never accepted her dad's help after her mom signed the divorce papers. They'd celebrated her sweet sixteenth birthday by moving back to Mom's hometown in southern Ohio. Mom returned to teaching and Amber took an after school job at her Uncle Warren's jewelry store. She paid for most of her academics by creating and selling custom jewelry like the bracelet she wore. She'd kept the bracelet to advertise her work and later as a reminder of the hard work she'd done on her own.

Approaching sirens and flashing lights drew her attention as two police cars pulled into the parking lot. They stopped with their lights pointed toward where she leaned against the truck.

Graham clicked his phone off as a woman officer opened her door and approached the two. He leaned close to Amber's ear. "I'll do the talking. I've identified myself as a federal agent, so no need to use the alias. We'll continue our conversation once we reach a safe place."

He pocketed his phone and flashed his federal badge as the black-haired female officer approached. "This woman is going into protective custody tonight, but her apartment has been ransacked. We need to see if the perps removed any items, and have her gather a few things. I knew your department would like to investigate first."

"Thank you for following the correct procedures, Agent C—"

"We're glad you arrived quickly, officer." Graham's voice cut off the policewoman before she said his name.

The woman's mouth twitched. She waved a hand between herself and the other policeman, "Officers Clara Hollingsworth and Matthew McCaleb at your service, sir. Let's see what happened inside." They walked toward the apartment, pointing flashlights at the broken streetlight.

Amber's anger burned. An hour later, she and Graham followed the two officers through her trashed apartment. Overturned statues she'd made in sculpture classes during her undergrad years littered the floor but seemed intact. Scattered books lay open on shelves and across the floor.

Stepping around tossed cushions, she headed to her bedroom where the chaos continued. Boxes normally stowed in her closet were on their sides with photos and mementos spread across the floor. The few pieces of clothing that still hung on their hangers were pushed to the side. One of the closet's folding doors leaned haphazardly against a wall.

Her childhood jewelry box sat open on her dresser. The few personal items she kept in the small cedar container lay in their usual compartments. The intruder must have been surprised that someone who specialized in jewelry only had a few sentimental pieces in her home. She'd sold the valuable pieces she created to pay for a college education and provide an income for a life free of her father.

At least they hadn't touched the family Bible sitting on her nightstand. She started to reach for it, but paused in case it needed fingerprinting.

"Is that the Bible you mentioned?" Graham's question broke into her thoughts.

"Yes, I don't think the intruders thought it would be important. They had their hands on everything else, though." She looked around her bedroom. A sense of desecration seeped into her pores and sent a chill down her back. Clothing dangled from open drawers, but she couldn't spot anything missing. She clenched her fists. Would her father's legacy continue to haunt her even after his death?

Graham turned to the officers and waved a hand toward the dust covering most of the surfaces in the room. "Did you find any fingerprints?"

"We found nothing. The intruder wiped everything clean, no fingerprints anywhere and that would include Miss Whitney's on file as an educator. They must have been here a while." Officer Hollingsworth stood in the doorway, her brow wrinkled with concern.

Officer McCaleb cleared his throat and looked at Amber. "When was the last time you were home?"

"I left early this morning to work in my new studio on Main Street. I've been putting in long days trying to get ready for the opening. Someone posing as an artist wanting to display their works in my shop called this afternoon. They asked me to meet them there tonight at 8:45, but they never showed. Guess that was part of the plan. Someone tried to attack me there tonight."

"Did you call it in?" Officer McCaleb raised his brows.

"No, Agent Graham showed up and kept them from kidnapping me." Frustration for not reporting the crime washed over her.

"Did you get a phone number for the person who asked about meeting you tonight?" The officer's hand hovered over an electronic tablet.

"It looked like a local number, or I wouldn't have answered. It should be on my phone." Amber reached for her empty pocket and frowned. "Graham has my cell. You'll have to check with him." She took her gaze off the policeman long enough to realize Graham no longer occupied the bedroom.

"Thanks, I'll check. In the meantime, you have our permission to gather a few things to take with you." The policeman lowered his tablet and left the room.

Her gaze focused on the old Bible. She wondered why Graham asked about having one earlier. She dropped the worn book into an emptied teacher's tote along with a pair of jeans, some tops, and several changes of underwear. She grabbed a hair clip from her dresser and pulled her hair into a short ponytail.

When she entered the bathroom to gather some toiletries, Graham stood in the way, taking pictures and texting them off to someone. She stared at the mirror he'd been photographing. Blood red letters, shaped from a tube of lipstick she never used, warned: *Give up the info.*

Amber muttered, "I would if I could." When she saw her current toothbrush swimming in the toilet, she elbowed Graham out of the way so she could fish through an open drawer for a replacement.

Graham picked up a tube of toothpaste from the floor and handed it to her. He grasped her arm and met her look as she reached for the tube. "Giving them what they want won't keep them from coming after you. It would only put your name further up on our suspect list."

"So you think I'm a suspect of what? I don't even know what information my father had." She ripped her toothpaste from his hand and started searching the vanity for her deodorant. She snarled over her shoulder, "Make yourself useful and get that toothbrush out of the toilet. You can leave it in the tub for now."

"How about I throw it in the trash instead?"

"Nope. Old toothbrushes make great art tools. Once that baby is dipped in bleach, I'll take it to my studio."

"And do what?"

"It will come in handy for the classes we're going to offer at the shop. Several artists, including me, are planning to teach there once the place has a grand opening. Maybe you should sign up for a course once my father's fiasco of a mystery is solved."

Graham shook his head. "God skipped over me when giving out artistic talent."

He pulled an evidence bag over his hands and transferred the toothbrush from the toilet to the tub. "Happy now?" After she nodded, he continued. "Speaking of the mystery, did you put the Bible in the bag with your things?"

"Yeah, reading from God's holy word is how I start each day. I've been using this old one for a while. It brings back happy memories of my grandparents." She rifled through her tote and pulled the book out. "Wasn't there something you wanted me to look up?"

"Your father gave me two clues as he lay dying. One of them came from a Bible verse. Something about stones and names—"

"Well, I can tell you for sure that 'sticks and stones may break my bones but words will never hurt me' isn't located anywhere in the Bible." She tried to laugh at her lame joke, but fear snaked up her back as she remembered harsh words between her parents before their divorce. Words could hurt worse than stones. Her father's divisive comments were one of the reasons she hadn't dated, ever. It was safer to take care of herself and not worry about hurts inflicted by anyone else. Having to rely on someone for her safety had gotten old, even after only a few hours of being in Graham's care.

"Listen, I know that old childhood proverb isn't in the scripture. I think Max said something about it being in Revelation. Does your Bible have a concordance at the end?"

Amber pulled the Bible closer and stared at him in surprise. "Ah, so we have a biblical scholar on our hands, who knows about concordances. Very good." She flattened the book out on the bathroom stand and flipped to the back.

He stepped near enough that his arm brushed against her side. An entirely new feeling flooded her body. Attraction? Not if she could help it. He'd only brought trouble since they met.

She leaned away from him and ran her finger down the index of biblical references. "There's mention of twelve stones representing the tribes of Israel, could that be what he was talking about?"

"I don't think that sounds familiar." Graham's touch on her back caused a rush of attraction to spread into her chest. She leaned closer to the book, ignoring the quaking reaching from her toes to her over-tired brain.

She moved her finger along the line of references. "Here's one in Revelation chapter two. It could be the reference you said might be in that book. The verse is about receiving a white stone with a name engraved on it. Only the person who receives the stone will know the name."

Her thoughts turned to the stones she'd turned into jewelry for her father last year. They'd all been white quartz, nothing worth stealing, and nothing worthy of her father's past tastes in expensive living. She certainly hadn't done any engraving of names in the settings she'd created. Amber started to move her fingers over other references when Graham's hand covered hers, sending another unwanted shockwave up her arm and straight to her betraying heart.

"I think that's the passage. He talked about sending white stones to family members and friends for Christmas gifts. Did you happen to get one?" Graham's hopeful expression softened.

His wide brown eyes made Amber swallow the emotion trying to take over her mind. The soft glint from groomed honey-blonde hair almost made her forget to answer his question.

"Uh, I got one of the pieces Dad asked me to make. I don't understand why. He gave no explanation other than making me promise to keep it safe and never give the piece away. I laughed but agreed. They were cheap stones, not worth stealing. He could have afforded diamonds and rubies, but he chose inexpensive white quartz."

"Did you do any engraving on the pieces?"

"No. I made them and he paid me well for my services, much more than I would have charged. I figured it was guilt money. He took the pieces away for a while and then gave the one back as a gift. I haven't even looked at the necklace since he dropped it off."

"Have you checked to see if the people who ransacked your apartment tonight took your necklace?"

"It wouldn't have been here in the apartment. All our dealings happened at my school office. My necklace is somewhere in my desk. I'm not even sure now where I stuffed it. Do you think we should go there tomorrow to find it?"

"We're going now. Grab your bag." He took her arm as she put the Bible back into her tote and attempted to match his stride from the room. "Officer Hollingsworth, please see to locking up this apartment unless someone from my agency shows up to investigate. We're heading out to get something at the college."

Amber pulled from his grip when they reached his truck. Her arm still stung. "Are you sure you want to go now? Campus security is pretty light this summer. After tonight's excitement, I'd rather go in the daylight."

"The sooner we solve this problem, the better. We're going tonight. I'll text headquarters and let them know where we're headed so they can send another agent to meet us." His voice was firm.

She sighed as she climbed into his truck and tossed her bag to the floor. Yup, this was going to be just like one of those horror flicks where the victims ran right into the arms of trouble. She whispered a prayer as he maneuvered away from her apartment and headed into the dark night.

~~~~~

The smell of burnt coffee and copy paper filled the silent college foyer where Graham hovered over Amber's shoulder. He watched her punch in the security code for the locked building. It was an easy one to remember, should he need it again, or if the other agent showed up in time to help. The door clicked open. They traveled through a long hallway and then turned down another.

His attention roved from her swaying hair to every corner of the corridor as they walked toward her first-floor office. When they reached her door she paused, keys in hand. Amber took a deep breath and briefly squeezed her eyes shut. She probably prayed her office would be intact when she pushed the key into the knob. The building seemed pretty secure. She shouldn't have much to worry about.
~~~~~

Disorganized chaos met him as the door swung open. "It looks like someone's been here too." He shook his head as she burst into laughter. He reached for her arm. "Maybe you should sit down while I look around. The shock of seeing your office like this must be affecting your emotions."

She continued to laugh. "No worries, it looks like it did the last time I was here. I actually keep a neater office than most of my colleagues." She sat down at the desk and pushed some papers to the side.

He bit back another comment and focused on the mess. "Do you have any idea where you might have stashed your father's gift in this chaos?"

"It's got to be in one of the drawers. Just give me a few minutes to sort through them." She opened a drawer and pushed slips of paper and gadgets into a pile. After finding nothing, she smashed everything back down again. She moved from drawer to drawer until locating a white stone pendant hanging from a delicate chain.

Graham rubbed his hands together. "Do you see anything engraved on it?"

"I can't tell without my equipment." Amber moved to one of the nearby shelves and opened a small toolbox. "Let me get an eyepiece to magnify the stone." She held a small black tapered cylinder against her eye and peered closely at the stone. "Nothing on the outside—"

"That's disappointing." Graham stuffed his hands in his pockets and looked at the woman as she fiddled with a small piece of metal on the side of the stone. "What are you doing now?"

"I made this piece as a locket. There's a place in the middle to put a small picture or another tiny memento."

His heart rate stumbled and then picked up. Would they find their clue inside the compartment? The split stone popped open. A picture of an older woman, who looked much like the one in front of him, appeared in the miniature frame.

"What do you know? He put Mom in my piece of jewelry. That was nice."

"Is that all? Maybe you should look behind the picture and see if there is something more."

A boom sounded from the end of the hallway. Deafening alarms pierced the air. He stood. She stuffed the necklace into her jeans pocket and joined him at the door to her office.

Graham's arm blocked the exit. "Is there another way out of here?" Lights flashing from the ceiling joined the pulsing security alarm.

Amber slipped under his arm and led the way out of the office. She closed the door and waved him toward an exit. They heard shouting and the rumble of feet heading in their direction as the metal door slammed behind them.

Graham kicked a flower-filled urn in front of their exit, hoping it would give them a few minutes. As they sprinted toward his truck, he hit the automatic starter button. The engine roared to life. When he pushed the unlock button, an explosion ripped his vehicle apart. They both staggered backward from the aftershock. Debris flew from the truck as the vehicle went up in flames.

"This way." Amber's tense voice broke through the roar as she pointed to an ancient brick fortress.

He allowed her to grab his hand and lead him down the stairs of the nearby building. Punching in another code, she led him through an unlit hallway and into a dark room.

The pungent odor of turpentine stung his nose. He didn't know a whole lot about art, but he knew enough from his younger sister's attempted oil paintings to feel sure they were in one of the art studio classrooms. His thigh bumped into a table as she grabbed his elbow and yanked him across the room. He stifled a gasp from the pain and heard her mumble, "Wimp." Hinges creaked as they entered some kind of storage room.

An interior lock clicked. He whispered, "Where are we?"

"We're in a changing room. Some of the classes use live models. Don't worry, our school only allows them to strip down to leotards and gym outfits. We have too many high school kids doing college credits these days to go any further."

"Too much information. Do you think we'll be safe here?"

"Not many people know about the entrance we used. I doubt anyone saw us. We can settle down here for the rest of the night. There's a stack of yoga mats somewhere in this closet."

"Once we find your mats, I'll give you a half hour to catch your breath. Maybe by then, we'll be safe to head out." He needed to get her to one of the safe houses in a nearby town.

He reached toward a wall and began searching the room's perimeter in the darkness. Graham bumped into something with multiple plastic pieces. A rattling sound broke the silence. He hissed, "What in the world?"

She snickered. "Sorry. I forgot to tell you about the skeleton in the closet. Mr. Bones is one of our top models. He works for free."

"Are you always this funny?"

"Only when bad guys are trying to chase me down for an answer I don't have. I need to sit down and rest once we find those mats."

He thought he heard her giggle as his hands wrapped around the sides of a couple mats. "I found them." Graham shoved one into her hands and placed his near the door. A slice of pale light pierced its way under the door. "You didn't happen to bring your eyepiece with you, along with a little night vision? I'd sure like to know if that necklace has an answer inside the stone."

"If you give me my phone, I might be able to take a picture and enlarge it."

"You can use mine. I turned yours off after I shared the text you got. I didn't want anyone to use it to track us." He touched his front pocket to make sure he still had her device.

"Good one, Agent. Now let me have your cell phone."

~~~~~

Amber blinked. Light pierced the room when he retrieved the device from his pocket and tapped the side button. She admired his shadowed cheekbones while he pressed in the code to unlock the phone. She moved her mat closer, took out the necklace, and sat down. Reminders of sitting around a campfire with friends warmed her thoughts. She'd never snuggled with a guy while watching a fire. If this was what it felt like, she sure would have enjoyed it, if her dad hadn't set such a bad example.

"You ready to get to work?" His question spurred her attention back to the stone.

"Sure." Thoughts of Dad's betrayal made her lean away from the Fed as he opened his camera app. She always managed to find something she didn't trust in a potential boyfriend. Amber hoped she did the right thing by trusting this man with her safety, and for solving the current mess her father left behind.

She snapped several pictures using the flash, praying the light wouldn't reflect under the door and out into the classroom. Graham must have sensed her worry. He leaned his yoga mat against the bottom of the door frame and moved next to where she peered at the jewelry with the camera. "Does your phone have a macro feature?"

"Yes, ma'am. Let me bring it up." He took the phone from her and switched the setting.

"You make it sound like I'm some old woman with your *ma'am* talk." She took the phone back and started clicking again.

"That's just good southern respect, ma'am."

She huffed.

"Are you finding anything helpful?" He leaned closer. For a moment she lost her concentration.

"Not yet. It might help if I knew what we were looking for, but I don't think the bad guys know either, since they haven't robbed me of anything." She flipped on past the few pictures she'd taken and noticed he'd taken several scenic shots. "Nice photography, Mr. Fed. I do believe you have an artistic eye after all."

"Call me Graham. What I do with my photography is my own business." He bent closer when she moved back to the pictures she'd taken of the locket. "Were you able to see if there was something behind your mother's picture?"
~~~~~

"I can't seem to pry it out. I forgot to bring my lapidary tools with me when we ran." Sarcasm leaked from her lips. She tried picking at the picture with the tip of her nail but couldn't pry her mother's likeness loose.

"Will these help?" He removed a tiny pair of tweezers from the end of a Swiss Army knife.

"Thanks, Mac--Graham, I'm glad to see you can make yourself useful." She held out her hand. "Let me open the rest of the knife and I'll see what I can do."

Before using his tweezers, she opened a small blade and pried up a corner of the picture. Graham hovered over her, shining the phone's flashlight where she could see what she worked on.

"Looks like something might be embedded in there. Hold the light a little closer while I see if I can pick it out with—"

Thump. The sound of a door slamming against a wall resounded from the nearby classroom. A man shouted, "Are you sure this is where to look? I don't see any evidence of them in here."

"It's got to be the right place. The trace on the Fed's phone says we're close. She's with him, for sure. Besides, they forgot to click the outside door closed. We got in here without having to set off another alarm."

Laughter echoed from the outer classroom.

Graham punched the off button on his phone and groaned, "Fed?" The sound of crushed glass and metal echoed through the room as he destroyed his device under his heel. Their hiding place went dark.

Amber snapped the locket closed, wishing she'd remembered to close the older building's door tight. She stuffed the jewelry and the closed knife back into her pocket. Graham grabbed her elbow and moved her to one side of the door. The knob rattled, followed by a kicking sound. His whisper sounded in her ear. "Grab a mat and be ready to push them out of the way. After that, run like crazy to—"

When his voice faltered, Amber visualized a map of the campus trying to think of safe places. "There's a small grove north of here. If we can make it past two more buildings, the trees might provide cover. The place isn't far from the police station."

A harsh laugh sounded from outside as the kicking on the door grew louder. "I hear muffled voices. We've got them this time for sure."

Amber took a step back from the door and bumped into Mr. Bones. The skeleton's rattling spurred on the attack against the door. The metal door held its ground, but the frame began to crack. A final kick brought the door down with a whoosh. Graham tackled the first man like a pro football player.

Amber threw her mat to the side and used the skeleton as a battering ram to push past the other man. As they moved into the classroom, she pinned the assailant against a table and toppled Mr. Bones across him.

When Graham yelled, "Run," she took off. Tables and chairs fell to the ground, accompanied by the high-pitched breaking and scattering of plastic pieces. Between Mr. Bones and Graham, her erstwhile abductors would travel through a minefield of debris. She sprinted down the hall and out an 'emergency only exit.' The alarm sounded at the same time Graham cleared the door, a few feet behind her. Strobe lights flashed. Campus security would receive the call and come to investigate if the few people on duty weren't already busy at her office building. Hopefully, that would discourage their followers for a while.

By the time they reached the cover of the grove, her side ached and her breath came fast. Beams of moonlight filtered through rustling leaves, giving her a glimpse of Graham. He pushed his hands through his hair and seemed barely winded as he walked further into the woods. She could tell something bothered him. Between his rumpled hair and the tense aura emanating from clenched fists, she was afraid to ask what bothered him-- almost.

"How did they know to track your phone, and where is your backup agent?"

Chapter Three

Graham hesitated, but knew the woman deserved to know his thoughts. It might make a difference in where they went after leaving the shadowed trees. "Those men wouldn't have located my phone unless someone from the agency gave them the information. We won't need to use my Jones alias anymore. I wonder if an agent even received my request for backup."

"Oh." Her expressive mouth formed the word then flattened as the implication settled in. "Do you think we're safe going to the police station tonight?"

"To be honest, I'm not sure. The two officers we met seemed pretty straight, but they knew we were headed to the college after leaving your apartment."

"Is there any chance you have a backup plan?" She slumped against a tree and inhaled deeply as her labored breathing slowed.

He'd pushed her hard from the moment they met, but she'd been a trooper. His training, along with a daily jog, gave him the stamina to keep moving during the last few minutes. Those moments felt more like hours right now.

"Do you know of a hotel or bed and breakfast around here we could head to? I've got enough cash for a night or two. That would give me time to devise a backup plan. You could get some rest after we take another look at that piece of jewelry you made."

Amber straightened and started walking without looking back. "It seems like I have more answers tonight than you do, Agent Graham. I know a place nearby. Do you have any solutions for getting us out of the mess we're in?"

He followed her through the rustling trees. There was no answer to her immediate questions. He had no way of expressing the betrayal warring inside his head. Who would have given his phone information to the ruffians who nearly captured them in the classroom building?

The phone Amber's father gave him when he acted as the man's bodyguard still sat on his desk at the agency. The government-issued phone they'd tracked tonight was one designated for him to use exclusively with the FBI for this case. He'd contacted his boss on the bureau cell after calling 911 when they were at her apartment. He puzzled through the people who knew about the device. Other than his boss, at least three other co-workers were aware of the phone. Who knew how many people in the technology department kept an eye on him, unless the local police had a connection after tonight?

Amber stopped at the tree line and surveyed the silent neighborhood. "Looks like no one's around. Let's head down the street right across from us. We'll go two blocks and then turn left down an alley. A colleague is traveling during summer break. Loretta gave me a key so I can water her African violets once a week." She patted her pant leg, which clinked with a key ring.

"Let's go." They jogged across the road. A tall hedge grew along the first yard's border. He led them behind those bushes until they reached the next home. Weaving between parked cars provided some cover. Shadows of neighborhood trees shrouded many of their steps.

Tall shrubbery growing along the edges of the alley shielded them until they reached a cottage with a fenced yard. The front end of a car peeked from the shadows of a large shed facing the alley. No door protected the vehicle from the elements. Amber stopped and entered a gate next to the rickety garage. They padded to the back door of the little house, and she opened the door with a key.

He stepped around her, speaking in a hushed voice. "Let me go first, just in case."

"No one knows I come here except the lady next door. The neighborhood has been pretty quiet when I water her flowers." Amber kept her voice to a whisper and followed him into the dark house, snapping the lock closed behind them. "Watch out for the—"

Graham swallowed a groan when he stubbed his toe on something heavy. He hobbled through a small entranceway and into the main part of the house.

"Maybe I should go first. There's an interior laundry room where we can turn on some lights without being seen from the outside." She stepped in front of him and grabbed his hand. "Sorry about my friend's antique door stop. You aren't the first one to trip over her grandma's six-pound pressing iron."

She led him around the room's outer edge and into a smaller space. He felt a loss when she dropped his hand, closed a door, and flipped on an overhead light. Strong scents from laundry detergent and dryer sheets assaulted his nose as he took in the white appliances lining one wall.

Once his vision adjusted to the bright light, he looked at the woman in his charge. Which one of them really held control? She'd taken the lead throughout most of tonight's chase. In the dark, she'd seemed unafraid. Her pale face and the way she leaned against the washer for support said otherwise. If he didn't distract her, shock would push her into further distress.

"Did you manage to hang on to your necklace and my knife?"

She frowned and stood taller. "Of course." She emptied her pockets and slammed the contents onto the top of the washing machine.

Good, his strong woman had returned, not that she was his in any way. Any thoughts of settling down with a woman needed squelching. He'd seen the heartache his brother went through while Graham's former sister-in-law complicated their world. He didn't need that kind of chaos in his already dramatic life. Solving this latest case and moving on to the next one should be his focus. Shoving his hands into his pockets, he stepped near to watch her work.

She expertly snapped the locket open and pried a small rectangular piece from the space behind where her mother's picture had once been located. Two small metal prongs stuck out from one side of the tiny ceramic block. A green paint stripe adorned the side opposite the prongs. "This seems familiar, but I'm not sure why." She held it up to the light.

"Looks like something off a computer's motherboard to me, or it could be a quartz diode for an older electronic device." He took it from her fingers and turned it over to see if he could spot any identification engraved on one of the sides.

"Wow, Mr. Fed, aren't you smart." She leaned closer.

Her breath tickled his ear, sparking emotions he had no desire to follow. "I told you to call me Graham. Take a look and see if this spot might show something engraved on the diode." He placed it in her hand and took a step back.

"All right, Graham, I think you might be right in your elementary deduction." She tipped the piece back and forth. "It's too small to read clearly, but there is something there. It might be a single letter, maybe an M." She wrapped her fingers around the tiny object.

Her face registered sudden recognition as she opened her palm back up. "When Dad first started his electronics business, he had a lot of these sitting around his shop in jars. I used to glue them into mosaics. I think he told me they were used in radios, but right now I can't recall exactly what he said."

Graham's thoughts returned to his time as Max's bodyguard. A memory of an early task crossed his mind. "How many pieces of jewelry did you make for your father when he had you make this one?"

"There were twelve in all. I have no idea what he did with the other pieces. He did ask me to create space in each item for holding a small memento. I understand now why he wanted that done. He must have added the extra compartment for the diode using his own limited skills or had someone do it for him. He had a steady hand for working in tight places, but I struggle to picture him working with jewelry."

Graham couldn't control the smile that spread across his face. He could at least take the lead on this part of the case. "When I started working as Max's bodyguard, one of the first things he asked me to do was take him to the post office. We mailed off eleven packages. Since it was December, I figured they contained Christmas gifts. He handed me the tracking information and told me to keep it safe if anything happened to him, so I could notify his closest friends and family."

"You wouldn't happen to have those papers on you right now, would you?"

He tapped the side of his forehead. "No, but I took note of the names and addresses. I've got a photographic memory. Give me your birthday once, and I'll never forget the date."

"Good for you. I don't want to remember my own birthday, much less anyone else's."

He waited. It didn't matter if she told him her birthday or not. He already knew the date from his investigation, but it would be nice if she offered the information. He almost missed her whispered reply.

"April first. No joke."

"That must be a pain," he said, to lighten the mood.

"Yeah, every April first I go into hiding from anyone who knows it's my birthday. I've had a few whacky gifts over the years." She frowned then put her hands on her hips. "Where did you put the original tracking papers?"

"Your father burned them after I told him I had the information memorized."

"Where do we go from here?" Her fingers tapped out a rhythm on the washing machine's metal lid.

"We'll track down the jewelry and then try to figure how the pieces of Max's puzzle fit together. Are you ready to hit the road?"

"Where are we going?"

He grimaced. She wouldn't like most of his answer. "There were several women from Max's failed relationships on the list, including your mother."

"Other women?" Amber looked confused.

He kept going. "There were also two men with family names you might recognize, Jethro and Warren."

Her face paled. "Do I need to let Mom and my uncles know they might be in danger?"

"I don't think anyone has this information but me. Back then the addresses didn't seem important to the case. No names of criminals were on his list of packages. It truly looked like Max sent holiday gifts to family and friends." He mentioned the other names, but Amber failed to recognize them.

"What do you think the pieces will reveal once we locate all the parts?" She hopped up on the washing machine and looked down at him.

The urge to squirm filled him again.

He would probably regret sharing what he knew, but she had a big stake in the operation since her safety was at risk. Until he figured out the mole's identity, she would be his only ally. He watched her closely to see how she reacted to what he had to say.

"Your father dealt with some high-powered cybercriminals. That's how he made much of his money for the last ten or so years. There were hints from underground sources that he decided to hand evidence over to the authorities and get out of the business."

"Really?" An uncertain frown crossed her face.

"Yeah, really, but he never followed through. I hinted that I might know a way out, but paranoia kept him from fully trusting me. He did step away from this world by whispering the verse from Revelation into my ear, so maybe that clue was his answer."

"Dad had a habit of stepping away when you needed him the most. He left Mom and me high and dripping in doubts about whether he ever cared for us. Before Mom received the divorce papers, he chose to move in with a younger woman from work. He'd been seeing her for a while. Leaving me with this mess doesn't surprise me at all."

"His demise gave him no choice."

"Death took the problems out of his hands and piled the troubles onto us." She sighed. "Do you really think he wanted to change?"

"I would like to assume he did, but I can't guarantee anything. He started going to church the last month I worked for him. We talked about some of the sermons. I took him to a few meetings with the minister but wasn't privy to their conversations."

"At least there's something to hope for. Maybe he made peace with the Lord before he passed. I don't wish the alternative to heaven on anyone. Mom and I grew closer to God after Dad left and we settled in her hometown. However, I wanted nothing to do with him. When he offered to help pay for college, I refused because I felt like he cared more about money than me. Though I hated how he rejected us for another woman, I eventually made myself pray he would change. It took a while to make that conclusion, but gradually my faith grew stronger. I still struggle to forgive and forget the way he deserted us."

"Understood. Speaking of forgiving, I'm having a little trouble right now forgiving whoever blew up my truck. We're short on transportation and we need to take a trip. Do you have access to the sedan in the garage?"

"Sure do. I've been starting the car when I water her flowers, so the engine will work well when Loretta gets back. Though, I'd hate to have it get blown up like your truck. My friend would not be happy." Her fingers rapped out another rhythm on the washer.

"We'd only drive her car for a short while, just far enough away to get a rental. Afterwards, we can leave her vehicle in a public lot at an airport. It would be safe there while we travel for a few days."

"Should we leave now? As tired as I am, I don't think I can sleep for a while. It'd be great if I could grab another to-go bag before we head out. I regret losing the old Bible, but I'm glad to be alive." Amber dismounted from the washer.

"We're not going back to your apartment. That's too dangerous. How close in size are you to the homeowner here? Maybe she has something in a different style that isn't like what you'd usually wear." He took a step back to avoid her close proximity.

"She might have what I need. Loretta's clothing is unique. She has a very artistic style." Amber snapped off the light and stepped out of the room, leaving him in the dark. He waited just outside the laundry room. Shadowed moonlight poured through a high window.

Moments later, she returned wearing a long top over her pants. A shawl or scarf draped across her shoulders. Something that looked like a large shoulder bag swayed from her side. He couldn't tell the exact colors in the dark but doubted they were subtle, definitely not her usual style.

"Ready, cowboy?" She plopped a hat on his head and jingled a fob and key in front of his face.

"Let's ride." He grabbed the keys from her hand and carefully made his way around the edge of the kitchen, avoiding stubbing his toe again.

As she closed the backdoor behind them and double-checked the lock, he surveyed the yard. The distant sound of a dog barking disturbed the night, but otherwise everything seemed normal. They stayed in the shadows as they approached the car. He used the key to unlock the doors. Using the fob would have set off an unwanted sound.

When he settled into the driver's seat, he located the overhead light control and twisted the knob until darkness once again filled the vehicle's interior. A temporary sense of safety filled his mind as they both put on seatbelts. The peace wouldn't last. Amber wasn't going to like their first stop.

Chapter Four

Amber gripped the console as Graham deftly wove through the neighborhood and headed for the countryside. She noticed how often he checked mirrors and fought the urge to do the same. A partial verse from scripture flittered through her mind. *Do not be anxious.* She had plenty to be worried about. Bowing her head and whispering a prayer for safety brought some peace. When she opened her eyes, she noticed Graham had angled the car back toward the northern edge of town where she'd heard her father lived the last year of his life. They approached a security gate locking off a development of exclusive estates from the rest of the world. Graham typed in a code and drove the car through the gates when the gap widened.

"I thought we were headed for an airport parking lot. What's going on?" Amber crossed her arms.

"Our first address is on the way. I thought we'd get the jewelry from there before we left town." He hesitated.

Teacher intuition told her he held something back. She gave him a piercing stare.

His shoulders sagged. "When we sent out the packages, I wondered why your father would mail two boxes addressed to his home. We're going to stop at his former house first and talk to the current Mrs. Whitney. She doesn't seem like the kind to wear the type of jewelry you made, no offense. I only hope she didn't throw the pieces away."

"None taken. As you well know, I didn't wear mine either." She frowned, wondering why the woman deserved two pieces of the jewelry. She'd refused to see the woman since Dad remarried years ago. The affair had cost their family. As a strong-willed sixteen-year-old, she'd put her foot down when Dad tried to contact her about visiting. Her mother's attorney friend said according to the laws in the state, she could make her own choice at that age. Amber hadn't wanted to look at the woman then. She looked down during Dad's funeral and harbored no desire to meet the woman, then or tonight.

After the divorce, Dad seemed glad to break off all ties. He sent a settlement check covering the purchase of a small cottage for them to live in. After Amber refused the college money, she'd not spoken to him again until he contacted her about the jewelry.

"I'll wait in the car while you ask her about the pieces." She looked out at the estates they passed.

The mansions seemed larger and larger with every twist in the road.

Graham braked suddenly. The car jerked to a stop as he turned off the engine and lights. "Something's wrong. The house should be lit up with spotlights." His hand pointed to a mansion sitting in the far curve of a cul-de-sac. Neighboring houses gleamed with exterior lighting.

The house directly ahead of them displayed a black silhouette against the sky. A dark sedan sat shadowed in the driveway. The small car looked out of place in front of a garage large enough to hold several expensive cars. More vehicles than any couple would need. She couldn't imagine Dad not keeping his house up with the proverbial neighborhood Joneses. He'd always maintained a proud exterior. Relief had overflowed when her father's pressure to be perfect became a thing of the past after the divorce.

"Stay here and lay low. I need to make sure they're all right." Graham undid his seatbelt and reached for the door.

"They?" Something didn't add up.

"Yeah, your stepmother and half-sister live here. He sent them each a package with the jewelry enclosed." Graham leaned back into Loretta's car.

"What?" Her mind froze. She had a sister and didn't know it. Suddenly it made sense that Dad hadn't seemed too torn up about losing contact with his older daughter. "I have a sister?" She clapped her hands to the sides of her face, feeling like she posed for the famous *Scream* painting. She wished she could let out a scream. Her head pounded as anger piled itself on top of the night's fear, and the adrenaline-causing roller coaster of events.

"You didn't know?"

"No." The urge to remedy her ignorance rose as she pushed open her door. "I'm coming with you, whether you like it or not."

"Suit yourself. You might be safer with me anyway." He closed his door and joined her in front of their vehicle.

Surprise that he didn't argue gave her a sense of control over the situation. She did not look forward to finally meeting the person she'd always thought of as the evil stepmother. But, the idea of having a sister made her want to go into the house like a mama bear and take out the evil that might be lurking there.

Her resolve faltered. They'd seen some awful things tonight. How would a young child hold up under the pressure? She fell behind Graham and prayed. *Dear Lord, help everyone survive what lies ahead of us.*

As they edged along the side of the house, Graham pointed to a power box with its cover hanging open. He didn't touch it. When they got to the back entry, a glass panel had been smashed in, leaving the door open for their entrance. A scream echoed from the front of the house, followed by the sound of a slap. Amber trailed Graham into the house, avoiding slivers of glass littering the floor next to the back door.

A woman's voice called out in terror. "I told you, I don't know about any secrets. Max didn't share anything from work with me since the day we married."

"Where's his daughter? The email said something about a daughter holding the key." The crack of another slap followed the man's low-pitched demand.

The sound of breaking glass rang from the front room. A whiny voice groaned, "Oow. What just happened?"

Another crash blasted through the house.

"Someone's throwing stuff at us. I thought she said no one else was here." The man continued his rant.

"Hey, you. Come downstairs now, or this woman isn't going to live much longer," the lower voice threatened from the front of the house. The creak of footsteps moving across wooden floors echoed from the front of the house and down the hallway where Graham and Amber waited.

Graham stood tall and shouted, "You're surrounded by law enforcement. Put your weapons down and step away from Mrs. Whitney."

Crash. Another breaking sound came from the front room as one of the men groaned.

"Thanks for the diversion, Officer J. I'm coming in for the arrest." Graham edged along the hallway. Confusion coursed through Amber's thoughts. Was there another security person on duty? Where was the sister he'd mentioned?

The woman shrieked again. They heard the thump of something heavy hitting the floor. The ensuing silence froze Amber in place. Seconds later, the echo of heavy footsteps headed away from their location, followed by what sounded like the front door slamming into a wall.

Amber joined Graham as they cautiously made their way toward the front of the house. Moans came from a semiconscious woman strapped to an overturned chair. Blood ran down the side of her face. Graham stepped to her side while Amber went to one of the front windows and peered out.

"The car is gone." She turned toward the pajama-clad female on the floor. Compassion for the woman overcame any hate she'd held. Her stepmother looked so young, much younger than expected. "Does she need an ambulance?"

"I think so. There should be a landline on the table by the sofa. The address is number seven Grand Court." He started to undo the woman's bindings. "I could use my knife right now to get these ropes off of her."

Amber removed the tool from her pocket, careful to not disturb the pieces of her dissected necklace. A rustle whispered above her head. Gripping the knife, she took a ready stance.

"Is that you, Mr. Graham?" A hushed, young female voice spoke from the second story of the mansion.

"It's me. You did well, Jade. Do us a favor and keep a lookout from an upstairs window for any more trouble." He took the pocketknife from Amber and loosened the ropes enough to pull the chair and binding away from her stepmother's bleeding limbs.

"Is she going to be all right?" The girl's voice wavered from above.

"I hope so, kiddo. We're going to get her some help. They may take her to the hospital to help her recover." Graham's voice sounded consoling. Amber watched as he removed an afghan from the couch and covered the shivering woman.

"Will you stay here with me if she has to leave?" The small voice grew softer and more childlike.

"We'll make sure you're safe." His vague answer made Amber figure they'd be adding a traveling companion for at least this evening. Would the stepmother become a part of their group too?

Amber found the phone and let the dispatcher know about the need for an ambulance at a break-in. She walked across the room with the portable phone and handed it to Graham so he could share health information.

Looking up, she saw the silhouette of a preteen girl standing near one of the upstairs windows. She had a sister named Jade. Guess Dad decided to give both of his children gemstone names. The girl must have been born within the first few years of her dad's marriage, if not the first.

Graham cupped his hand over the phone. "Maybe you should go up there with her. You might need each other right now." He raised his voice. "Hey, Jade, I'm sending up a friend. You two have a lot in common."

Amber felt her way up the stairs, making each movement as purposeful as she could. Both their lives were about to change. "Hi, Jade, my name is Amber Whitney."

"Oh." The girl hesitated and then threw her arms around Amber. "You must be the sister I was never allowed to meet."

"That would be me." Amber returned the embrace and then stepped back to hold a younger reflection of herself at arm's length. The resemblance was uncanny, other than lighter-hued curly hair, which reflected the light of the moon shining through a window. "I never knew about you."

"I never heard of you either until Daddy decided to go to church a few weeks before he died and now —" She looked over the railing at the woman sprawled on the floor below.

Sirens and flashing lights pulsed from outside the house.

Graham shouted from below, "You two better hide until I figure out what we need to do next."

Amber followed Jade into an upstairs room where the younger girl led them into a closet. Clothing brushed the tops of their heads as they huddled together and waited. Jade sniffled. Amber wrapped an arm around her sister's shoulders. Moments later, the lights flickered on in the room outside of their closet. An alarm briefly sounded and then grew silent.

"Do you really think Mama Julia will be okay?"

"I think she will." Amber couldn't promise more. The girl's mother had moaned but she knew no other details. The name Jade used didn't seem right. Her father would never have allowed her to call a parent by a first name.

Jade seemed to gain some strength from the half-assurance. She wiggled out from under Amber's arm. "How come you're here in the middle of the night with Mr. Graham?"

"First tell me why you called your mother Mama Julia."

"She's only been my mom for the last year, but she's been the best I've had." She crossed her arms and jutted out her chin. "Now, you answer my question."

Amber chewed her lip to keep from reacting. Dad had a way of messing up more than one life. She wondered how many hearts he had broken but chose not to ask. Now, they were all in danger because of his secrets. "Our father sent two pieces of jewelry to this address. A white stone would have been the main part on them. Do you recall seeing the pieces?"

She watched recognition spread across the child's face. Jade lifted her foot in the air, revealing an ankle bracelet with the white stone dangling from its circle.

"I have Mama Julia's matching wrist bracelet. It has a white stone too. She didn't think it was worth much, so she gave it to me. Daddy didn't seem to care. He only asked that I not lose the bracelets. I'm not into bracelets on a wrist, so I let Olive wear it."

Jade exited the closet and headed for a dresser covered in small stuffed animals. She lifted a long-eared puppy from the pile. The bracelet hung around the toy's neck. Amber debated about whether to laugh or cringe. Instead, she leveled with her sister.

"Graham and I need to look at these. We will get them back to you afterward. Right now, it's a clue in a puzzle we need to solve. Once we know all the answers, you and your Mama Julia will be safe."

Jade pulled the wrist bracelet from the plush pup and handed it to Amber, along with the one from her ankle.

Graham entered the room. The girl ran to his side and gave him a hug. He looked at Amber and nodded when he saw the bracelets in her hand. "I see Officer Jade has come through with several pieces of evidence."

"Yes, sir, what's the status downstairs?" Amber felt the urge to add a salute but stifled the movement because of the seriousness of the night's events.

"They're taking Mrs. Whitney to the hospital for the night. Officers Hollingsworth and McCaleb responded to the call and promised to provide protection for her until this is all over."

"Do you think you can trust them?" Amber's voice threatened to crack under the stress.

"I don't have much choice to do otherwise." His shoulders sagged. "They were still finishing paperwork at your apartment when their colleagues responded to tonight's college events."

Doubts still wormed their way across Amber's mind as her sister clung to Graham's arm. "Where will Jade stay tonight?"

"I told the officers we'd take care of the kiddo since she can't go to the hospital alone. If she went with Julia, they'd call in child services. I don't think Jade would want a stranger watching over her." He held up a fist and Jade gave it a bump.

"Can I help you solve the puzzle?" The child's adoring face looked up at her hero.

"We'll see. Right now, we just want to keep you safe." He tightened his side hug. His affection for the girl was obvious.

Amber noticed a selection of small purses hanging from the side of the dresser. "You would be helping us a lot if you picked out a purse to carry the jewelry. We've got several baubles we need to find before this is all over. You could be the guardian of the gems."

Graham nodded his approval. "Pack an overnight bag, kiddo. You can't stay here. We have some driving ahead of us."

"Gucci."

"I don't care if the bag is Gucci or big box, just pick something." A fleeting shaft of envy stabbed Amber, who bought her accessories at discount stores.

Jade rolled her eyes. "Gucci means cool, sis." She snagged a quilted floral bag and held it close as she twirled in place. She paused. Her gaze searched the room. "What about my house? Can't we stay and protect it from the bad guys?"

"The community security guards will make sure the house is safe for the night. We better head out." A frown creased his forehead.

Amber picked up a thin Bible sitting near the stack of stuffed animals. "My Bible went missing tonight. Would you mind if we brought this along? It may help us with some clues."

"Sure thing, but I've got the whole thing on my tablet." Jade lifted a medium-sized device from her bedside table.

"No tablets. We need to go without a way for anyone to trace our movements." Graham paced across the room and stood outside the door. Amber watched the girl stuff things into a bag. Memories of packing her own bags long ago pulled her back to another time. Her thoughts wandered to the different homes she'd lived in with her parents as a child. Each place had been bigger than the previous one, none as filled with grandeur as the one she stood in tonight. As a child, she'd come to the point of expecting the moves along with changing schools and friends. She'd learned to be happy making acquaintances. She rarely chose close friends she would have to leave behind with the next move.

Once Jade had her bags packed, they headed for the stairs. Graham switched off lights as they made their way below and out the back entrance. When they arrived at her friend's car, Graham inspected the vehicle before they climbed in and drove away from the cul-de-sac.

Amber watched Graham punch in the gate code once again. A realization popped into her mind. "Whoever attacked Mrs. Whitney must have known the code."

"It would appear that way." He signaled and pulled out onto the northbound street. She leaned back in her seat and peered down the road. Miles later she heard her sister's breathing lengthen into sleep. Amber relaxed into the seat and prayed until she fell into unconsciousness.

~~~~~

"Great, we've got company." Graham's voice forced her to struggle from her slumbers. She rolled her head from its cramped position and pushed herself upright. The reflection of headlights blazed from the side mirror. Someone followed them and drew nearer. Graham swerved onto a side road and increased his speed.

"I thought you said we wouldn't damage my friend's car." Amber grabbed her armrest as their speed increased.

"I'll do my best. That choice just got taken out of my hands. I'm not sure how they found us but they did." The car behind them tapped their bumper. Amber couldn't control her scream as her sore arm bumped against the side door. A frightened whimper came from the backseat passenger. Graham gripped the wheel, keeping them on the road as the other car backed off and then attempted to pass them. Amber stared at the black sedan. It had to be the same people who'd been at her father's house. The passenger window opened and someone in a ski mask waved a pistol their way, shouting for them to stop.

Graham shook his head and for a moment it looked like he would try to outrace them. As the other car sped to match his speed, he slammed on the brake. The other car shot forward. He put their vehicle into a spin. As they spun, their bumper connected with the sedan and sent it careening toward an electric pole.
~~~~~

Amber heard a thumping sound and looked in the rearview mirror. A flash erupted from the transformer dangling above the sedan resting against the swaying pole. Sparking wires illuminated the dark night, dancing through the air as arcs of energy snapped and popped. She prayed the electricity would keep the men inside their vehicle. Her back pressed against the seat as Graham sped from the scene.

"That was definitely Gucci, Mr. Graham. My heart is pounding like when I ride the giant screamer coaster. Maybe you can teach me how to drive like that someday." Jade leaned forward and stuck her head between the two bucket seats.

"I hope you never need those skills." Amber leaned back and placed a hand on her pounding chest.

"We only got a few scratches on the car." Graham made one turn and then another. "I'll make sure your friend gets it back with all the dents smoothed out."

"I should hope so." She peeked at the side mirror, seeing only darkness. As she watched road signs come and go along their way, regrets from tonight's car damage overflowed Amber's conscience. Thanks to Dad, her world had suddenly become very complicated. Their lives were in danger over a bunch of quartz stones, and now she had a sister in the mix. Dad managed to hide her sister's existence and information about a bunch of felons from his estranged family. Now they were fleeing from unknown attackers who busted part of her friend's bumper. She huffed loudly. "Are we going to change cars soon?"

"We should be within a half hour of the airport. There's an independent car rental I've used before. They'll take my cash and send us on our journey after we check this ride into a long-term parking facility."

A deep sigh came from the back seat where her younger sister appeared to be slumbering. Hopefully she'd have sweet dreams instead of nightmares from the last few hours.

"What about Jade?"

Chapter Five

Graham stared at the road ahead. They didn't have much choice. "Jade will have to come with us until I can figure out who we can trust."

"How about trusting me with a few more details of where we are headed? You told me yesterday that my father shared two clues with you. I know we're trying to locate the jewelry. What was the other clue?"

"He kept mentioning that Alabama was the last place he wanted me to ever go. That's why our travels will mostly be from north to south. We are going to be visiting Max's relatives and friends who now have the quartz stones. Our last stop will be Gorge Bluff in the eastern part of that state."

"That sounds like Dad. He didn't want anyone to know about his roots in the South. Gorge Bluff is close to his hometown. After Granny passed away, we never went there again."

He watched Amber fiddle with the bracelet of multicolored stones hanging from her wrist and stare out the window before she continued. "I had some of my best summers sorting the colorful quartz rocks that filled Granny's driveway. Some were white stones like the ones I used for Dad's jewelry. Most were oranges and tans with a few black stones mixed in. I laid those pebbles out in patterns in her flower beds. Granny even bought a stone polishing machine from her youngest brother's hardware store. We turned some of the shined stones into my first attempts at making jewelry. Uncle Jethro put some of my work out to sell in his hardware store. I think he and Granny bought all of my wares." A brief smile crossed her face. "Those were precious times."

"Maybe your father is sending you communication about the past. I hope that message also contains the names we need to close down the cybercriminal operation your father became part of." Graham tapped the steering wheel, wishing he'd been able to obtain the information sooner.

She swiveled toward him. "I wonder if he was trying to send a message to the other recipients of my jewelry. Do I know who they are?"

Her stare brought a yearning to get to know the cute woman better. Graham cleared his tight throat before answering. "Your Great-Uncle Jethro Whitney in Gorge Bluff, Alabama, will be our last stop. Other than that, I doubt you will know any of them unless you kept up with all his ex-wives. There are several unrelated names on the list. Did you ever hear of a Mary Belle Crackenbush from Georgia?"

"No, do you know who she is?" The frustration in her voice matched his concerns about the case.

"She's the only one Max said anything personal about in my presence. She was his Sunday school teacher when he was a young man. Her words of faith finally started to sink in during the last month before he died. Unfortunately, she also passed away recently. We'll try to find her contacts in Northern Georgia and hope they haven't discarded the jewelry."

"So we'll get to visit your home state." She tapped his arm, sending a hint of attraction to his heart.

"It's a peachy place to live." Graham turned on his blinker and eased up a ramp, trying to ignore his reaction to her touch.

Amber snickered at his attempt at humor. He pulled out onto the main highway near the airport and moved up to the posted speed limit. Jet engines roared above their heads as a plane began its flight and lifted into the air. The plane soared across a pink-shaded dawn sky, and then disappeared into the clouds. Familiar signs pointing to the airport's long-term parking lot appeared just ahead. Graham signaled and entered the automated gate. He grabbed the ticket and parked.

Jade yawned loudly, to the point it sounded fake. Hopefully she hadn't heard the details of their journey. "Are we there yet?" She poked her head between the front seats.

"Not by a long shot. We need to trade rides, so grab your bags and follow me." Graham led them down a side road and across an alley before they emerged at another lot, full of rentals.

A lone man sat in a booth at the front of the family-owned lot. He nodded when they entered and pushed a form toward Graham. "We have your usual SUV available if you'd like it, or you can have something more family-friendly since you brought your ladies with you."

"Do you have a van with some power?" Graham didn't correct the man's assumption about Amber or Jade. The less people knew, the better. He regretted not having them hide out while he rented the vehicle.

"I've got a luxury one over there with plenty of power and fancy seats for your gals." The man grinned and pointed to the vehicle parked near the front of the lot.

Graham reached for his wallet. "We'll take it."

"Would you like that on the card we have on file?" The man pushed back his baseball cap and turned toward an ancient computer.

"No, this is for personal use." He passed the man enough cash for more than a week's rent and insurance. He held up some extra bills. "I don't need anyone knowing I was here. My ladies need some time away."

The fellow mimed locking his lips and winked as he pocketed the extra cash. "Thanks, man. I'll have to take the wife out for dinner next weekend. There are perks to owning your own business. Have a good time."

They loaded the few possessions they carried into the van. Graham drove out of the parking lot, searching the road to make sure no one followed them. Light gleamed through Amber's side of the vehicle when they turned onto an interstate. The early sun made her brown hair glow with all kinds of highlights. He looked away from the intriguing woman and attempted to focus on the road.

"Where are we headed first?" Amber shielded the side of her face and looked his way.

"I put all the addresses in order, according to distance. The closest is just north of the state line in Michigan. After that we'll head south. Hopefully, by the time we get back into Ohio later today, Julia will feel well enough to take care of Jade. If that doesn't work, I have a friend who can keep her safe while we continue our search." Graham signaled and passed a slow-moving vehicle.

"Can't I go with you two? This is like a real live video game with car crashes and bad guys chasing us all over the place." Jade's pleas ended with a pout strategically reflected in Graham's rearview mirror.

"I'm glad you're having fun, Jade, but this is the real deal and you could get seriously hurt. You'd be much safer at home." Graham pulled back into the right lane.

"Yeah right, like I was last night." Jade's voice rose as she made a valid point.

Graham looked in his mirror and saw Jade's crossed arms and hanging lip, big enough to leap from for a dive into a pool of tears. "Sorry about that, kiddo." He yawned and rubbed a hand across his face. "You're right about last night, but we'll have to see."

~~~~~

Amber took a look at the handsome man's exhausted face. "Maybe I should drive while we don't have a tail." Her short nap, along with the change of vehicles, gave her a boost of energy.

"That might be a good idea. Just stay on the interstate until you get to Michigan's exit 17. Head west from there. You'll get to a little village about ten miles out. Wake me up when we arrive, and I'll help find the place."

He pulled into a rest area parking lot and they did a quick rotation. Graham stretched out across the back seat while the two sisters claimed the front. Amber settled into the leather driver's seat. The scent reminded her of a tooled purse she'd bought at a second-hand store when she'd been into carrying a bag. It felt good to symbolically be in the saddle and do something useful. Graham's snores soon filled the van.

"I hope I didn't snore like that when I was sleeping," Jade said.

"No, you were as quiet as the moon up high. At least while I was awake." Amber concentrated on the light traffic flow. Not many
~~~~~

commuters competed for the road at the moment.

"I'm glad we finally got to meet last night." Jade leaned sideways on the door and gazed at her sister.

"I am too. I'm sorry our father neglected to let me know about you. However, I pretty much dumped him when he left Mom and me for a new wife." She signaled left and passed a slower car. "I'm not sure if that woman was your mother or one of the other wives of Max. I guess that would depend on your age."

"I'm twelve, almost thirteen. I'll be a teenager in another month." The girl straightened in her seat, sitting as tall as she could muster.

"Then the woman my father married after Mom would have been your birth mother." Amber tried to keep the resentment out of her voice, but knew she hadn't when Jade replied.

"Sorry. I didn't know my real mom very well. I had a nanny who took care of me until I started school. I still sometimes text with Nanny Joy."

"I'm glad you had someone who cared for you." Amber held her feelings at bay. She'd never had to worry about her mother's love, only her father's.

"Yeah, my mom cared more about going to work than being at home. I think she liked working better than Dad did. They fought a lot about their jobs. She worked for MAX, along with Dad. I ignored them and played with my toys and Nanny Joy, until it was time for kindergarten. When I started school, Dad started trying out new wives."

"How many wives has our father had?" Amber tightened her hands on the wheel and prepared for the worst.

Jade grew quiet and started counting on her fingers. "If you count yours and mine, there were five. I hoped Mama Julia would be the last wife since she's nice. I guess Dad dying took care of that." The girl paused before continuing as she picked at the design painted on her nails.

"After Dad married Mama Julia, she was in a car wreck. I guess she got to thinking about nearly dying, so she decided to go to church. I liked going to church with her and then Dad. For the first time in my life, I had some friends I was allowed to visit." Jade hugged one of her knees to her chin.

Amber nodded. "That's good. I didn't make many friends, either, when we lived with him. We kept moving to bigger houses. It was hard to hang on to friends. Mom and I became involved in a church after we got out from under Dad's control. She returned to her faith, and I accepted Christ a year after we moved away." She sent a grateful prayer heavenward, thankful for the faith she'd grown to love.

The younger girl stifled a yawn. "How long have you known Mr. Graham? He's quite a hunk."

Amber choked out an agreement as warmth coursed up her neck and into her cheeks. "Uh, we've only known each other for about twelve hours."

"Wow, that's not long. Just wait 'til you go somewhere with him. I got a lot of attention from the girls in my church group when Dad gave him permission to take me to an event."

"I'm sure you did." Both sisters rode in silence as their riding partner slept in the back seat. Amber watched the roads, glad to see only a few drivers traveling down the road ahead of them. Her sister's eyelashes rested on her cheeks. The girl's fingers periodically rattled out a rhythm on the console between the two of them. She jumped when Jade spoke again.

"What's up with the bracelets? It must be something really awful for those bad guys to beat up Mama Julia."

"I don't know everything. What I do know is that Dad put a clue inside twelve different pieces of jewelry he asked me to make. By the time we collect all the jewelry, those clues will solve a problem for the good guys, like our sleeping hunk in the back seat."

Jade giggled. "He's a pretty Gucci hunk."

Amber took note of the mile marker along the highway and started looking for their exit. "The pieces of jewelry were sent to individual addresses, which only Graham knows at this point."

"Are we headed to get one of them now?" Jade wriggled in her seat.

"You are one smart kitty." Amber signaled and exited off the highway. The sun rose higher, brightening the azure skies overhead. She lowered the visor above the windshield. Reflected sunlight in the rearview mirror made her squint, even though they headed west. Wishing for the sunglasses that sat in the console of her left-behind car did no good. Driving with one hand and shading her face with the other would have to work for now.

The snoring stopped from the back seat when they made the turn. Graham sat up and put his hand on her shoulder. A tingle of something she wanted to ignore spread out from where his hand rested.

"Let's pull off and get some gas," he said. "Both of us could probably use a break and some caffeine before we head for our next stop."

Two minutes later, Amber pulled up to a pump. She and Jade headed inside to grab snacks and drinks for their travels. Graham filled the tank and then met them inside the convenience market. After taking a bathroom break, they returned to the car.

Graham stood by the open driver's door and pointed to a huge store sitting behind the gas station. "It might be a good idea to stretch our legs at the wilderness store over there. I'm pretty sure they have a cheap satellite phone I can purchase."

"Maybe we can purchase a souvenir tee shirt for Jade so her name-brand clothes don't stand out on our mission." Amber stretched against the other side of the van before opening the passenger door.

"Really? Gucci, or should I say cool for my ancient sibling to understand? I don't think any of my parents ever allowed me to dress in that kind of shirt." Jade vaulted into the car and buckled up.

"Our main man might need a change of clothes, too, since we may be on the road a few days." Amber winked from the front seat and then felt warmth creep up her neck.

"Ladies, we need to watch my budget." Graham put a hand over his chest.

Amber giggled. "I've got enough to buy each of you a tee shirt in my cell phone's wallet, if you hand my device over, chief. You're on your own for your satellite phone or whatever spy gear you need, Agent Graham."

Jade gasped. "I thought you were a bodyguard. Are you telling me you're some kind of secret agent?" She leaned as far forward as the seatbelt would allow.

"Thanks, Professor, now the whole world will know unless we swear our junior agent to secrecy." While his words held humor, his tone did not.

Amber squirmed in her seat as they drove across the mega store's massive parking lot. "Sorry, Graham. I don't think you have to worry about it being a secret anymore, since both the enemy and law enforcement know the truth."

"So I'm running all over the country with a Fed and a professor?" Jade's voice bubbled with excitement.

When no one answered Jade, she leaned back in her seat for the short ride across several acres of black pavement. An hour later they hit the road with bellies full of buffalo burger biscuits, a sat phone in hand, and new tee shirts for all.

<div align="center">~~~~~</div>

When they arrived at the little town west of their shopping spree, they made their way to a quiet upper-middle-class neighborhood. Well-manicured yards and shade trees lined the avenue where they parked. After they got out and stretched, the trio walked up a sidewalk to the front door and used a knocker made with a brass lion's face. When the door opened, Jade gasped.

"Mama Rita!" The girl immediately stepped behind Graham, who introduced his group and their purpose.

"I see you brought the brat along with you."

The woman's unwelcoming expression made Amber angry. She glared at the woman with one of her best teacher stares. The ex-wife hesitated. Then she gained her composure as she turned her full attention toward Graham. She put on a flirtatious smile as she led the agent into her home and sat next to him on an overstuffed loveseat. The sisters followed and sat across from the pair on a matching couch. Amber asked about the jewelry.

"No, I don't know why my ex-husband sent me the little trinket. He owed me diamonds for what I went through when we were married. Instead, he only gave me enough money to buy this little house. The alimony barely pays for my daily needs. I would have tried to sell the bauble if it hadn't come with a handwritten letter full of promises."

"What did the letter say?" Graham asked.

"He promised that if I kept it safe for a year, he'd make sure I had plenty of money to buy new furniture. He knew my weakness for redecorating all too well."

Amber noted the luxurious couch and chairs where they sat. Expensive knickknacks filled tabletops and shelves around the room. It would seem that the alimony provided well for the woman's needs and wants.

"If my memory serves me right, it was a brooch. Give me a minute to find it." She left the room and returned with a large jewelry box. She lifted out small divided boxes and paused to admire several of the pieces. "Oh, look, here it is. How much are you going to pay me for it?"

"Look, we don't have a lot of money or time. We just need to look at the brooch. You can have it back after we examine the jewelry in private." Graham's voice sliced the air with impatience. He stood and stepped away from where the ex-wife sat.

The woman placed a hand over her heart. "I suppose you can take it. I'll never have a use for the trifle since Max won't be around to buy my new furniture or send me alimony." The woman fanned her face and fell back against the loveseat.

Jade rolled her eyes.

Amber almost snickered at Jade's expression and the overdone acting. "Are you all right, Mrs. Whitney?" She forced a concerned look onto her face and moved next to the former Mrs. Whitney. She sat in Graham's vacated seat and patted the older woman's hand.

"I'm just mad at Max for kicking the bucket. I guess I'll be looking for a new husband or if worse comes to worst, a job." She held the brooch toward Graham. When he reached for it, she placed the jewelry in his palm and wrapped her hands around his. "Are you a single man, Agent Graham?"

"Thank you for the brooch, ma'am," He pulled away from her and stuffed the jewelry into his pocket. "We need to be going." He wrapped his arm possessively around Amber's waist as he pulled her up from the couch and escorted her toward the door. Laughter bubbled up from Amber's chest. His arm around her waist felt like it belonged there, leaving her confused.

Jade led their way toward the exit. She peeked out a windowed panel in the door. "Hey, that looks like one of Dad's business cars sitting out front."

Chapter Six

"Get away from the window." Graham pulled Jade to the side.

Were the henchmen randomly checking out people like ex-wives with a connection to Max, or had they somehow traced them to this location? Another option might be that they were making contact with this Mrs. Whitney to settle up any last alimony payments. Somehow, he doubted handing out money was involved, but he needed to give them the chance to prove otherwise.

He peered out through the sheer curtains from several feet back from a window. The men had gotten out of the dented vehicle. One of them walked near Graham's rental. The other walked up the sidewalk toward the house. They were about the same height as the men who'd attacked them the night before. Without their ski masks, he recognized them as MAX Enterprises employees he'd seen once or twice before.

"Mrs. Whitney, I'm going to trust that you will do the right thing. We're going to go out your back door when these men knock on the front one. If they ask about us, tell them we are gone. Understand? You do us right, and I'll make sure you have a date with someone when this is all over." He forced himself to smile and wink at the disgusting woman.

With a grin of her own, she fluttered her eyelashes, straightened her dress, and moved toward the front of her house. Graham would send his widowed boss for a follow-up interview with the woman. Maybe the boss would let him live to tell about the exchange.

Graham led his charges out the back door. They cautiously made their way along the side of the house. When they heard Rita Whitney open the front door, they plastered themselves against the wall, listening through her open screened window.

"Hello, gentlemen, whom do I have the pleasure of meeting today?" A picture of the woman flirting with the enemy flew into Graham's thoughts. Rita was probably fluttering her eyelashes like a butterfly.

"We're looking for your ex-husband's child," a familiar low-pitched voice growled.

"I haven't seen her in a while. She was such a bother."

Graham saw Jade's fists tighten as she listened. Amber placed a comforting hand on the girl's wrist. Jade didn't need to hear the woman put her down.

"We know she's around here somewhere. Max put one of those

tracking devices on her phone. Our boss's computer guy figured out how to activate it today. She's got to be close by along with a woman we've been following."

"Well my goodness, if you handsome gentlemen want to come in and check out my place, feel free to do so." The syrup in Rita's voice gushed like a fountain.

The sound of feet tromping into the house sent Graham's trio scurrying for the van. He pulled away from the curb, and then mashed the pedal to the floor at the edge of the neighborhood.

"I thought I told you no electronics." Graham had to force the words out from his clenched jaw.

"You only said no tablet. I put my phone on airplane mode. I thought that would be good enough." Jade's answer made him squeeze his fingers tighter around the steering wheel. There'd likely be a dent left from his anger.

"Apparently airplane mode did nothing to stop the tracking device from working."

"Sorry." Jade's voice was quiet.

"Give your phone to Amber. Now." Graham bit back an angry comment.

Jade pulled her phone from her pocket and disconnected ear buds hidden beneath a mass of blonde curls. She handed the cell to her sister. In the rearview mirror, he saw tears pouring down her cheeks.

"Do you know how to disconnect the tracker?" Amber's question gave the girl one more chance than he would have offered to make things right.

"I have no idea." Jade's voice cracked.

"Throw it out the window, Amber." There was only one way to take care of the problem in Graham's way of thinking.

"Sorry, Jade." She lowered her window and tossed the phone into a farmer's field.

No one spoke for several minutes as they sped down a rural road. Fields of foot-high corn filled their vista, along with several white farmhouses and red barns dotting the flat landscape with dabs of color. All he saw was red.

"What's done is done. Is there a plan for what we are going to do now?" Amber's soothing voice broke into his growing frustration.

"We're going to go somewhere no one can find us until the sun goes down. Then we're heading for my friend's house, so he can provide a safe haven for Jade." This journey of theirs had no place for the child.

"What about Mama Julia? Can't I go back to her?" Jade's voice shook.

"You would only be putting her in more danger than she can probably deal with right now. Our pursuers seem more interested in you two daughters, than in Julia."

He wove his way through a maze of country roads until spotting a small campground. Graham paid for a spot near the back of the park and left the girls sitting in the van while he paced in front of the site. Only a few campers were around, and they parked near the front. Good, his mind needed plenty of space.

This little adventure kept getting more complicated. He should have checked to make sure Jade followed directions. She could be a rebel at times, as he had learned during his brief tenure as her father's bodyguard. That dangerous oversight was his fault. The rest of their situation, he could blame on Max's lack of trust that now endangered so many people. His agency entrusted him to get the information at all costs. Jade needed to be in a safe place until this mission was finished, one way or the other.

He pulled the satellite phone from his pocket and called fellow agent and friend, Carlton, to make arrangements for Jade's safety. Carlton and he had been like brothers. If there was anyone he could trust to not be a mole, it was the man who had been with him from his first day of training until they'd parted ways for this last mission. Carlton had recently been given time off to recover from a wound to his leg. His sister's ranch in the middle of nowhere would be the perfect hiding place.

Graham always kept his word. He'd follow through, but he would have to guard his heart when it came to the child and her beautiful sister. They had become a key part of this investigation.

After he let off enough steam, Graham headed back to the van. While he was gone, Amber had dissected the three latest pieces of jewelry and came up with more diodes to add to their puzzle.

"Here, Jade, as guardian of the gems, you can keep the jewelry. Two of them are yours. I don't think Rita will mind if you have hers. I'll keep these little guys." She had placed the diodes into a small pouch purchased at the wilderness store. Graham hoped she'd transferred the diode from her own piece into the bag. Her pendant still dangled from her neck.

"What are they?" Jade asked.

"We're not sure, other than being part of something electronic that our Dad cooked up." Amber pulled one out for her sister to inspect.

"Hey, ladies, did you find anything out from the latest clues?" Graham watched as Jade turned his way with a sad expression.

Amber's voice broke his focus away from her sister. "Nothing new, they're similar to what we already have. There are different colors painted on each item. That may prove important once we have all of them. I spotted letters on each one, but they don't seem to spell any words."

"I'm really sorry, Mr. Graham." Jade's head hung down to her chest.

"We can't change the past. You don't have anything else on you like a watch, or portable game?" Graham knew his voice was harsh but thought the girl needed to hear his feelings regarding what she had done. "No."

"Good. I don't know about the rest of you, but I need to doze off for a few minutes. We'll take turns watching and sleeping." He lifted the hatchback of the van and lowered the two back seats. The surface wasn't very soft but at least he could stretch out his six-foot frame and get some much-needed rest. The quiet sounds of female voices lulled him to sleep.

~~~~~

After sunset, they left the campsite and headed south until they crossed the Michigan-Ohio line on a narrow country road.

"Do I have to stay with someone I don't know? I promise I won't cause any more problems." Jade's pleas buzzed in Graham's ears like a pesky fly.

"Yes, but it will be for your own protection. I think you'll enjoy the place." He paused, trying to think of something positive to say. "My friend, Carlton, has an injury from an assignment he went on. He's recuperating at his sister's horse therapy farm. I'm sure you can probably sweet talk your way into riding while you are there."

"Okay, but I still wish I could stay with you two. I just met my big sister and I want to get to know her." Jade placed a hand on each of their shoulders.

"We'll find time to visit when this is all over. I want you safe so that can happen." Amber reached around and patted her sibling's hand.

"What about you, Mr. Graham? I don't want to lose you to the bad guys." Jade heaved a big preteen sigh.

Thank the Lord, Amber jumped to his rescue.

"It will be easier for him to watch out for one of us at a time. Besides, I know a few things about self-defense. I might need to take care of him if he gets in trouble."

They spent the rest of the ride laughing about taking out the criminals who tried to abduct Amber from her store and on campus. An hour later, a sign for Heavenly Horses Therapy Park welcomed them as they turned down a long drive. A porch light gleamed from the front of a large ranch house with a wheelchair ramp leading up to the front door.

Graham pulled the van in between the house and barn. "This is your stop, kiddo. It won't be too bad of an experience for you."

"I guess." Jade slid from the vehicle with slumped shoulders and followed them up the ramp. A horse nickered from the barn. Her footsteps quickened, and she made it to the door before Graham knocked. "Do you know what kind of horses they own?"

As Jade asked her question, the door swung open revealing a blonde-haired man and woman. Graham's friend leaned on crutches. Colton's sister smiled.

"Welcome to Heavenly Horses Therapy Park, Jade. I'm Tamera and
~~~~~

this is my brother, Carlton. We're looking forward to having you visit." She shook Jade's hand. "We have all kinds of horses, from thoroughbreds to rescues."

Graham reached for his friend's hand and nodded to Tamera. "Good to see you both. This is Amber Whitney and her younger sister, Jade. Thank you so much for agreeing to take care of Jade for a few days."

"You're all welcome to stay for a while." She smiled at the group.

Her brother interrupted, "But, we understand that duty calls. We'll make sure Jade has a good time while she's here." Carlton pulled out his wallet. "How are you on cash?"

"I could use a loan and a different vehicle since we're going off grid. The people who followed us checked out the van at our last stop." Graham was grateful for his buddy understanding their situation and thinking ahead.

"I'm glad I can at least do something while I'm out of commission." He handed over a wad of cash and SUV keys. "Take care of yourselves. My vehicle is out back."

"Thank you, we should be on our way. Somehow, whoever is after Max's information keeps finding us. We should move on before they figure out a way to follow our trail to you."

~~~~~

Amber watched as Tamera waved them into the house.

"At least come in for a little while. I can pack up some sandwiches for you to take." The woman smiled at Graham.

A weight seemed to drop onto her shoulders. What kind of relationship did he have with the perfect blonde welcoming them in and offering to feed them? If Amber felt starved before, she wasn't now, at least not hungry for what this beauty offered.

"What man can refuse a picnic packed by Tamera?" Graham looked like he was being lured in like a wide-mouthed fish. The woman had looks, she had food, and she had therapy horses.

"Tell me about your horses." Amber needed a change of subject. "Will Jade get a chance to ride while she is here?"

A smile crossed Tamera's face at the mention of her animals. "Definitely. All of our horses are gentle and perfect for anyone's experience level. Even my boyfriend can handle riding on my animals."

"Gucci, I can hardly wait." Jade followed the woman over to the bar dividing the kitchen from the great room of the western-themed home.

Even her sister seemed enamored by this perfect woman. Amber followed them and sat on a bar stool, too exhausted to offer Tamera any help preparing the food.

Her jumbled thoughts rambled back to what the woman just shared about the horses. "Did I hear you say you have a boyfriend?"
~~~~~

"You sure did." Tamera's eyes lit up.

Amber felt lighter after hearing Tamera's affirmation. Yet there was no real reason for her to feel jealous. This situation wouldn't last much longer. She'd never see Graham again after they solved the case.

"What's this about our Tamera dating?" Graham joined the conversation and stood behind Amber's stool. His hands brushed her shoulders, and then he removed them like he'd been shocked by the same stab of electricity that coursed down her back. It was the wrong time of year for static electricity. Her emotions had played an unwelcome trick.

Carlton hobbled closer. "Yup, Martin Johnson came to check on my recovery a few weeks ago. He kept making excuses to come back. It didn't take an Einstein to notice he cared more for Tamera than he did me."

Graham stiffened next to Amber. "How well do you know the guy?"

Carlton shrugged. "Reasonably well, the man has worked as an independent technology consultant for the agency off and on for the last five months."

"I don't think I ever met him." Graham frowned.

"You've been undercover for six months. I doubt you would have seen him."

"Let's keep it that way. No one needs to know our connection to Jade."

"I don't think you have anything to worry about. We became acquaintances since the investigation that took me down. He seems okay except for being a real nerdy kind of guy." Carlton leaned on the counter and snitched one of his sister's cookies.

"Clark Kent was a nerd, and he turned out to be a superhero." Tamera stuffed sandwiches, chips, and cookies into a sack and shoved them across the divider. She slammed two caffeinated beverages down next to the bag and turned her attention to Amber and Graham. "You two seem good together. Maybe we should be asking you questions instead of harassing me about my friend."

Graham lifted his palms in the air. "We're just trying to solve a case."

His ready reply reinforced Amber's need to squelch the interest she tried to fight off. He clearly held no interest in a relationship. She only played a part in finding the answers he sought.

"Our biggest concern is there may be a mole in the Ohio office. For Jade's safety, I hope it isn't your friend."

"I'm sure you don't have to worry about him. He's not at the agency often." Tamera's mama bear look rivaled any teacher's glare Amber ever experienced.

Amber shrugged and picked up the bag of food. "Thank you for the picnic and for taking care of my sister." After hugging Jade, they climbed into Carlton's white SUV.

Amber prayed for her sister's safety as they drove off into the night.

Chapter Seven

Graham finished off the last of a caffeinated drink and set the can down in the console. They'd have to stop soon for a break. Back roads and small towns didn't boast any rest areas. He needed to find an alternative. As he drove through another rural village, he spotted a not so big, big-box store. A few cars sat in the small store's well-lit parking lot. He pulled in and turned off Carlton's SUV. The big-box name blared across the night sky in bright letters.

Light streamed through the window and illuminated Amber's heart-shaped face. Even asleep, she looked exhausted. At least she didn't appear upset like she did when Tamera turned the focus to their relationship.

The usually confident Amber had remained silent since then. He hadn't felt much like talking either, at least out loud. His mind kept replaying Tamera linking them together as a couple. Amber looked sweet and innocent in her slumbers. They both sighed.

He had to stop thinking about her. She would let him down at some point, just like his ex-fiancée. He bumped her elbow. "Wake up. I need to take a break." Interest and attempts at distancing warred in his chest. He leaned away. "We're getting out here. Time to wake up." He rattled the drink can in the console and repeated his summons to take a break.

"Where are we?" Her dewy eyes held his attention for a moment as she yawned. Her outstretched arm brushed against his.

Graham pulled away like he'd touched a fire, and maybe he had. He needed to answer her question instead of fighting temptation. "We're somewhere in the middle of Ohio."

She looked at the dashboard clock. "It only takes a few hours to get from one end of Ohio to the other. Are you going in circles?"

"No, I've been taking the back roads to keep anyone from following us." He focused his gaze on the store.

She stretched and looked at their surroundings. "I see even big-box stores can come in small packages."

"And very convenient locations. I thought we could both use a break and maybe pick up some snack food. Take your time shopping. We're not too far from our next stop. Just in case there's trouble, I'd rather get there in daylight in order to scope out the situation before we ask another person about Max's jewelry."

They got out of the SUV and headed for the store. When they entered, a sleepy greeter popped up from a chair near a row of carts. "Morning, folks."

Graham tipped the cowboy hat Amber had loaned him from her friend Loretta's house. He'd held on to the head covering when they leased the rental. It helped hide his identity to a point. The style was growing on him. He placed his hand under Amber's elbow and hustled her into the store when she started to reply to the greeter. "Let's go, dear; we don't want to keep your aunt waiting."

"Sure, honey." She was a quick learner. "Should we grab a cart?" She wiggled out of his hold and started shopping. They swung through the canned meat and fruit aisles after selecting a loaf of bread and some tins of nuts. Amber grinned at him as she picked up a can of chunky chicken. "I lived off of this kind of stuff when I worked my way through college. No refrigeration needed and it sort of meets your basic food groups. The little containers make good sorting dishes for art supplies too."

"If you say so. I try to eat a little healthier fare normally, but I see your point." He headed their cart toward the restrooms in the back of the store, where they took turns waiting with their items. While she used the facilities, he looked through the nearby book aisle and snagged a Bible. They'd left Jade's copy with her at the horse farm. The volume wouldn't replace the well-worn one that had blown up in his truck, but it felt good to at least provide some comfort for the woman who'd been a trooper through the last day or so of their unexpected journey.

Once they were back in the SUV, Graham moved the vehicle to a somewhat darker spot in the lot. He pushed the cowboy hat over his face. "Time for some more shut-eye."

"I'm tired of sitting, cowboy. You enjoy your nap while I take a stretch." Amber's hand rested on the door handle.

"Not on my watch." He pushed the hat back up to the top of his head and reached over to prevent her from getting out.

She removed his hand and glared. "Get over yourself and take the nap. I'll just do some stretches beside the car. I understand the need to be careful."

"Okay." Graham shoved the hat back down. He didn't like what she wanted to do, but needed at least a few minutes rest, before he passed out. He'd almost begun to trust the woman, if that was possible. Closing his eyelids, Graham concentrated on trying to relax.

~~~~~

Early morning sunlight filtered into the SUV's back seat. Amber lay on her side, using the light to read her new Bible, open to Psalm 23. She needed the words about walking through the valley of the shadow of death. Lifting her heart to the Lord, she had just started praying for a safe day when Graham jerked his seat upright.
~~~~~

"Where is she? She promised not to go anywhere."

"I'm right back here, Mr. Grouch." She held back her laughter.

She barely heard his muttered, "Sorry." She closed the Bible and put on her shoes without acknowledging his half apology.

"Are you ready to meet stepmother number three?" Graham planted the cowboy hat back on his head.

He seemed to be enjoying the headgear better than her company.

"No, but it doesn't look like Dad gave me much choice." She got out of the car and walked around to the passenger's side. She closed her eyes and faced the morning sun for a few minutes before taking her place in Carlton's loaned SUV.

A half-hour later, they drove past the address on Graham's list. All was not quiet on that front. Tables covered with folded clothing and household items of all sizes lined the driveway. People milled around looking at yard sale merchandise. Furniture for every household room littered the front yard. A poster board attached to the mailbox proclaimed, "Getting Married Sale, Everything must go." Amber had never heard of that kind of sale before, but she'd been surprised several times in the last few days. A shapely middle-aged woman chatted with the customers who were looking at everything from coffee tables to jewelry.

"Oh no, you don't think she's sold the piece of jewelry before we got here, do you?" Amber's heart took a dive.

"Let's hope not. We better get out and take a look. Maybe we'll be lucky and locate the piece, then get out of here without anyone making a connection." He pulled into an open spot a half-block away. They wove their way back toward the house, dodging between people walking away from the sale carrying lamps and piles of clothing.

Amber stepped around several tables before spotting a tub of inexpensive jewelry. Snarled chains dominated the items. Some pieces looked broken. She ran her hands through the tangles and finally spotted a white stone choker wrapped around a charm bracelet filled with floral figurines. She grabbed both and headed toward the woman and her cash box.

On the way there, she spotted a big floppy hat. Maybe she needed something to hide behind like cowboy Graham. She grabbed the headpiece and got in line to pay for her items. Amber studied the ex-wife in front of her and wondered what the lady had seen in her father. A wave of pity for anyone bearing her father's name as a wife filled her soul. She was glad the woman had found someone new.

"Congratulations on your wedding."

"Thank you, dear. I see you picked out a piece from my ex-husband. He asked me to keep it safe while he lived. Now that he's dead and gone I have no use for his cheap little choker. I hope you get more use out of it than I did. The charm bracelet holds much better memories. Enjoy." The woman stuffed Amber's purchases into a plastic grocery bag and smiled.

"Thanks." She nodded and turned away. Graham lingered nearby, perusing a stack of books. Several women shoppers looked his way. Some bumped elbows with a friend and smiled. So much for not being too obvious. The man drew women's admiration like a flower did a—

Bang. A shot rang out. Graham crouched and held his arm. People screamed and ran for their cars. Amber heard rushing feet behind her, and then someone grabbed her shoulder.

"This time don't make it so hard. We want whatever you've been collecting from the ex-wives. Just give it to us and—"

She lifted her elbows and twirled into her attacker. She saw more than one blonde curl as the man covered his bloody nose with his hands. She didn't pause to take in his features. The sound of another bullet ricocheted through the air. At first, she couldn't see Graham, but then she heard his voice call from behind a sofa in the middle of the yard.

"Head for the SUV. I'll be right behind you."

Graham dodged behind a wooden dresser. Another bullet dusted up the ground near his running feet. His life seemed more in danger than hers. The attacker had indicated they wanted whatever she had purchased at the yard sale. Hoping that they would not shoot at her, she ran to a piece of furniture near Graham and stooped down behind it. She pulled the jewelry out of the sack and ripped the charm bracelet away from her white stone creation. She put the white stone choker around her neck and tucked the floppy hat under her arm.

Dropping the charm bracelet into the grocery sack, she stood up and shouted, "Everything you need is in the bag." She'd put the crooks in the bag if she could. No shots rang out. Amber dropped the bag on top of a wooden table with a clunk and hurried toward Graham. Together they ran for their ride.

Amber grabbed Graham's hand. Moisture seeped across her fingers. She looked down and saw his blood covering her hand. "Looks like I'm doing the driving."

"Just get us away from here. I'll be okay once the initial shock wears off. I don't suppose you had any defensive driving classes in your past?"

"Nope, but hopefully I can at least drive away before those guys figure out I gave them a handful of flowers."

"Huh?" Graham's voice reflected pain.

"Never mind, hand me those keys." Frustration filled her voice.

"Push the button on the dash with your foot on the brake and put her in gear." He groaned.

"One of those kinds of cars?" Amber scanned the dashboard looking for the button.

When he didn't answer, she did what he said. The engine roared to life. She set the SUV in motion. He wrapped a hand around the bleeding wound and moaned when she pulled away from the curb.

Amber reached into the console between them and stuffed a tee shirt into his hand. "Use this to apply pressure." She turned a corner and refocused on the road. "Should we go to a hospital? Maybe the police could meet us there."

"I'm pretty sure the bullet only grazed me. I've had a similar wound before. We'll need to get some bandages and antiseptic once we're in a safe place." His voice sounded stronger.

"So where do we go from here?" Amber pressed harder on the gas pedal once they cleared the neighborhood.

"We're headed to your mother's next. For now, just take a southbound road."

"Great. That guy back there said something about finding us because we were visiting all the ex-wives. I don't like this one bit. According to Jade's count, that lady back there at the yard sale is the last ex, except for my mother and — What about Jade's birthmother?"

"She didn't receive a package from Max. Don't know why." His eyelids drifted shut.

Amber hoped he hadn't lost too much blood. Mom had always been a good hand at healing. She'd know what to do for Graham if Amber couldn't help before they got there.

Thoughts of Mom being hurt any more than she already had by Dad's actions ground their way into Amber's thoughts. She glanced at the settings on the dashboard. The car pointed south as Graham had suggested. Sooner or later, they'd cross Interstate 70 and could take it to 75, then south to Mom's house. Graham moaned. She pushed the pedal down and headed for the fastest way home.

An hour later, signs for the interstate glistened in the mid-day sun. She pulled into one of the convenience stores near the major road and parked. Her hands shook as she pushed the button to turn off the car. Grabbing the satellite phone from the console, she stepped out of the vehicle and left Graham sleeping against his door. It looked like he was resting comfortably and the blood no longer flowed. She willed her fingers to stop shaking and punched her mother's number into the phone. Hopefully Mom would answer the unknown number.

"Joe's Grill, what would you like to order?" Mom's familiar voice chirped with merriment.

"Very funny, Mom. It's me, Amber. I'm using someone else's phone."

"I'm sorry, sweetie; I didn't recognize the number and thought we'd have a little fun."

"We?"

"I've got some company." Mom giggled. She hadn't giggled in a long time. Something was up. "I don't know if you remember Harold Duncan from work, but we've been seeing each other the last few months."

"That's wonderful, Mom. Look, I need you to get out of your house and head somewhere else. Dad has messed up our lives again. I'll explain more when I see you. For now, I need you to pack a bag and go to a safe place. There are some really bad people who may come looking for you. If Dad sent you any jewelry with a white stone around Christmastime, please take it with you."

"I know exactly where the jewelry is located. I only accepted it for your sake and something he promised. I'm grabbing it now, and we're heading out the door after I grab my overnight bag." Amber heard her mother explaining the need to leave, her words muffled, probably by her hand over the receiver. "We're going to head over to Harold's place. His house is the only Cape Cod on Glenberry Avenue."

"Take care of yourself. We're coming your way soon." Amber's shoulders relaxed. Mom was safe for now.

"So you have a 'we' too? I'm glad to hear—"

"It's not like that, Mom. He's protecting me right now. Look, I've got to get off this phone. We'll see you in a little bit." Amber pushed the phone into her pocket and started to go into the store for first aid supplies when she realized her wallet was still in Graham's possession.

The leftover cash from the yard sale wouldn't cover bandages and meds. She needed to wake him up for more cash. She knocked on his window and he opened his eyes. No man deserved to have such sweet eyelashes, but he did. A slow grin crossed his face as he blinked those beautiful lashes. She jerked the door open. He groaned in pain as he half fell out of the SUV. She pushed him back upright.

"I need my wallet or some cash for bandages. Looks like a little pain medicine might be in order, based on your miserable groans." Amber crossed her arms and waited.

He straightened and looked around as he pulled money from his wallet. "I see we made it to the interstate."

"Yup. After you're patched up, we're heading for Mom's friend's place as fast as this baby will take us. I already called her and told her to go to a safe place."

"Good. Grab me some coffee while you're in there. I'm having a little trouble waking up." He leaned his head from side to side, stretching his neck.

"How's the bleeding? You seem awfully tired." She fought the urge to reach out a comforting hand.

"I'm good. Just don't take too long."

Amber's gut rolled as she watched him release his seat belt and rest his head against the dashboard. She headed for the store, intent on being as quick as possible.

Chapter Eight

Graham stepped out of the vehicle and leaned against it for support. The thought of coffee sickened him, but he needed a moment alone to pull himself together. He fought to keep from losing his balance as his head spun and nausea crept up his throat. He'd kept his eyes closed during the drive, praying for their safety, and hoping she'd not notice how much pain radiated from his wounded arm.

Once the whirlwind in his head settled down, he pulled her bloody tee shirt away from his skin. He fought the desire to scream like an alley cat. The crease was deeper than he'd let Amber know. Graham owed her a new souvenir shirt, and more. She'd been an excellent partner throughout this whole fiasco.

"Hey, tough guy, let's get you cleaned up." She set his coffee in the console cup holder and opened her sack of supplies.

Graham leaned against the side of the vehicle and allowed her to cleanse his wounded arm. It burned like crazy. He flinched as she ran several wipes over his arm. She moved closer and her hair brushed against his chin, sending another kind of fire straight to his heart. As he ran fingers from his good hand across her hair, she looked up. A sweet blush filled Amber's cheeks. His hand moved to her chin. Her lips parted. Then she shook her head away from his hand and looked down.

Her voice shook. "Let's get this wrapped up in bandages and head out. We can't let those men hurt Mom." Her words sounded stronger at the mention of protecting her mother. "I got another cheap tee shirt for you to wear. The one you've got on looks like a tie-dye project gone wrong."

Under the shadow of the SUV's open door, Graham wriggled out of his bloody shirt and pulled the new one over his head. "You got me a superhero shirt? Really?"

"It was all they had in anything that looked remotely like it might fit your incredible hulk. Besides, you just proved you could survive a speeding bullet. What can I say?"

Graham studied her body language. "Are you nervous?"

"Yeah, how can you tell?" She stepped away and then climbed into the driver's seat.

"When we first met you said something about being a comedienne when you were under stress." He watched her adjust the visor and prepare to drive.

"Who's stressed? We've only got bad guys chasing us, cars blowing up, a mother to rescue, and you're bleeding. No biggie and..." She paused, lowering her voice. "...and I don't want to lose you." She swiped at one eye as she pulled from the station and headed for the interstate ramp.

"Agreed. I'd hate to lose you too. I need your help to solve this case. We have to focus on finding all your dad's clues."

Amber huffed. Guess he said the wrong thing.

Good, he needed to put a wall between them emotionally. Graham closed his eyelids on the pretense of resting. She knew where they were going better than he did. He hoped they could avoid their enemies while she drove.

The memory of touching her hair and wishing he could kiss her swirled through his thoughts like a school of tiny fish. He had no plans to ever marry. He'd only be playing with her emotions if he followed through with a kiss. She was too sweet to inflict that kind of harm onto. Past experience with the ex-girlfriend taught him not to get close.

Amber was clearly a hometown girl. She'd expect a husband to come home every night in one piece, not bleeding from a gunshot wound. He had to give her credit; she'd handled his wound without flinching and held her own against attackers. Her only reaction to the stress so far had been in the form of an odd sense of humor.

His ex had been pretty uptight about her desire for living the white picket fence, "honey, I'm home" lifestyle. Neither he nor his brother had been able to satisfy her expectations. When the woman dumped him for his brother, it had driven a wedge into the heart of their family.

His mind drifted back to Amber's perky little nose covered in freckles and her naturally pink lips. She was an appealing person beyond those looks. She'd proven herself as a friend, a sister, an artist, a Christian, and now as a car-driving nurse. She seemed flexible enough to accept the imperfect. The woman had even cried a tear over the thought of losing him. He felt his lips turn up in a smile. Maybe someday, when he had a desk job—

"You okay over there, sleeping bear? You look like you just won a race or maybe a pot of honey."

"I'm thinking honey, and it will taste mighty sweet once this case is solved. I'll be glad to get back to a normal assignment." Graham attempted to cross his arms and groaned. He shifted his weight away from the sore arm and shut his mouth before saying anything else that might encourage her interest.

~~~~~

Amber pulled into a rest area, not far from the exit to her mother's hometown. She turned off the engine and studied the man sitting next to
~~~~~

her. He'd almost kissed her back at the store. She might have welcomed it, but, in her experience, men only brought trouble, and she needed to keep that in mind. After all, her father was the whole reason for the mess they were in. Dad had been married to his job more than to any of the women he'd taken as brides, based on what she'd learned in the last twenty-four hours. Agent Graham also seemed like the type who would place job over family. He'd made that clear with his last comment about looking forward to his next assignment. He indicated it would be sweet to finish with her and Dad's mess.

She needed to keep her head on straight. She had a business to get off the ground and an apartment to clean, thanks to this Max mess. Still, she couldn't resist taking a minute to study his handsome profile. He looked good in his superhero shirt, too good. Heat clambered up her neck and into her cheeks. A snort came out through his nose and then he fell back into deep breathing.

Graham truly seemed to be resting. He hadn't touched the coffee he'd asked for back at the convenience store, so she'd swallowed every drop of her not-so-favorite beverage in an effort to stay alert. This stop, to empty the bladder before going into a scene of unknown danger, was required. She hated to wake Graham while he rested peacefully. She thought about leaving him snoozing while she went in, but realized she might need whatever help he could provide when they got to Mom's friend's home. At the very least, he'd need to be alert enough to call for the police. Feeling a little bit ornery, she poked him in the ear.

"Good afternoon, Mr. Superhero, time to wake up and save the day." She snickered when he slapped at his ear. Then regret rolled over her like a steam roller. He'd used his sore arm and now leaned over in pain. "Sorry."

"I bet you are. So, why are we stopping? I thought you were in a hurry to get to your mom's house." He rubbed his sore arm and looked out the window at the rest area.

"I drank your coffee and it came back to haunt me. Besides, if I have to kick box the enemy to save Mom, I can't do it with a full bladder. We're almost there and I want to be ready for anything."

"That sounds like a wise move. We'll both go in. Meet you back here in five." Graham managed to climb out of his seat on his own. He waved her ahead as they both headed for the restrooms.

More than five minutes later, Amber paced the sidewalk in front of their SUV. It was tempting to go into the men's room looking for him, but she didn't want to embarrass her superhero. Not hers personally and never would be, but he did give off a good superhero impression. She stretched against the side of the vehicle, wishing she'd asked him for the key fob. At least she'd be out of the hot sun, and not out here pacing where everyone was probably wondering what she was doing.

A familiar sedan with a banged-up bumper and side pulled into a parking space several spots down. No, it couldn't be. She slid along the opposite side of the SUV and crouched down, praying they hadn't seen her.

Running footsteps approached. "Well, who do we have here? This seems to be my lucky day. We were hoping to meet up with you at your mom's house. This will do since there's no bodyguard to save the day. Did you leave him in a hospital somewhere?"

Amber stood and backed away from the man who wore a hat pulled low enough to shadow his face, but not cover his blonde curls. There was something that bothered her about the curls. Now wasn't the time to think about it. She whirled to run but strong arms grabbed her from behind and swung her legs up in the air. As she struggled, she screamed and kicked out at both the man in front of her and the one behind.

The blonde man pulled something from a plastic bag and pushed it toward her face. She got a whiff of sweetness. Her head began to spin. Great, they were going to knock her out. She shook her head to the side and whimpered, "Help," as her body grew weaker.

~~~~~~

Graham shook his hands under the hand dryer. He felt much better after his nap. No blood seeped from his wound. He took that as a good sign he would recover. Stretching his limbs, while waiting for his turn in the crowded bathroom, helped too. A busload of college baseball players had been ahead of him. He'd chatted with a couple of the guys about their stats for the season as they waited in line. Amber probably thought he'd gotten lost. The dryer cut off, and the sound of shouting rose from outside the building. A chill shot down through his core as he hurried from the restroom. He saw several of the young men he'd spoken with start running toward his SUV.

Two men held Amber between them. Her body hung limply in their arms. Desperation filled their faces as they looked at the large group of young men rushing toward them.

"Hey, man, just put the lady down. It's obvious she didn't want to go with you." Other voices chorused their agreement with the spokesman. "We just called the cops. They'll be here soon."

Helplessness filled Graham. He'd left his gun secured in the glove compartment when Jade joined their journey. He hadn't wanted the child to have access to the weapon. It would have been too conspicuous with the tee shirt he wore. With an injured arm he was defenseless against the men. At least the crooks' weapon hands were busy trying to hold onto Amber.

The group of ballplayers closed the circle. The two would-be
~~~~~~

abductors looked at each other.

The blonde man nodded. "We'll set the woman down if you let us leave. Have we got a deal?"

"Put her down. We'll watch to make sure you're good for your word." One of the athletes glared at the criminals.

They lowered her to the ground and backed away toward their vehicle. Moments later, tires squealed as they peeled out of the parking lot. Graham looked to see if he could read the license plate, but a shadowy cover obscured the numbers. The sedan did resemble the company cars owned by MAX Enterprises. It was definitely the one that had been following them.

Graham pushed his way through the crowd. "Thanks guys, she's with me." He leaned over Amber. Her breathing was normal. A white rag on the ground reeked of sweetness. They'd tried to kidnap her and had almost succeeded. Thank the Lord for the guys on the baseball team. He missed working with his team at the agency.

Amber's eyelids partially opened. She moaned, "Graham?"

"I'm here, and so are you, thanks to my new favorite team. Thanks again, guys."

"No problem, man." Several of the college men shook his good hand before heading back to their vehicle.

Sirens screamed as a state trooper car and an ambulance pulled into the rest park. Graham stayed by Amber's side until he'd shared his badge with the trooper and given the brief information that she was under FBI care. The medics from the ambulance looked Amber over. Her vitals all checked out, other than being slightly groggy. She'd only gotten a little of the anesthetic into her system, thanks to her struggles, and the actions of the bystanders.

After inspecting Graham's wound, the medics suggested they follow up with medical care. Both refused the offer of a ride to the hospital, saying it was urgent for them to leave right away. He only hoped the crooks didn't have enough of a head start to ambush them in Amber's hometown.

Chapter Nine

Graham steered the SUV down the exit ramp and into the small town where Amber's mother lived. A groggy but awake Amber sat up in the passenger's seat and directed him to the street where her mom said Harold lived. The modest Cape Cod looked well cared for. Trimmed bushes and an assortment of red, white, and blue flowers lined the beds in front of the home. A curtain opened and the familiar-looking woman in the window pointed them toward the side of the house. Amber visibly relaxed, and Graham did, too, after seeing Amber's mother was safe.

As they drove into the driveway next to a mid-sized blue pickup truck, the garage door rolled up. A gentleman sporting a white Santa Claus beard waved them inside. Once they parked next to a green compact car, he closed the garage door and waved them toward the entryway to the house. Graham offered Amber his good arm, and they followed the man.

"Welcome folks, I'm Barbara's friend, Harold. I know Amber, but I've not had the pleasure—" A welcoming smile spread across his face.

"My name is Graham, sir. I'm with the FBI." He offered his free hand in friendship and tried not to cringe as he felt the man's firm up-and-down motion pull against his wound.

"Thank you so much for warning us. Barbara's neighbor called her earlier and said someone was prowling around her house. Mrs. Rudolph called the cops on them, and they left when the sirens sounded." Harold opened a door and pointed their way into the house.

They entered the kitchen through a laundry room, and Amber pulled away to fall into her mother's arms. "Mom, I'm so glad you're safe." The women hugged for several seconds.

"Thanks to you, but you're not looking so good right now. Come in and have a seat before you collapse." Barbara Whitney led her daughter into a comfortable-looking living room where they sat together on a brown plaid couch. Graham and Harold hurried to keep up.

"Thanks, Mom, just a little run-in with the bad guys. They tried to drug me, but I'm feeling better now that I know you are safe." Amber leaned closer to her mother as Graham stood awkwardly to one side.

"Oh dear, Harold, get this girl some caffeine." Barbara Whitney's voice demanded action. Harold turned toward the kitchen.

"Actually, my stomach is feeling a little queasy right now. If you have any ginger ale, that might be better for what ails me." Amber placed a hand over her mouth.

"Coming right up. Graham, would you like to help me in the kitchen?" Harold's expression implied they should give the women some privacy, so Graham followed him.

"Looks like you've put Amber and her mother in quite a bit of danger." Harold frowned as he filled a glass with ice and poured ginger ale slowly into it. His displeasure seemed to sizzle as much as the carbonation releasing from the drink.

"I can't take credit for that danger, sir. Max Whitney, Amber's father and Barbara's ex-husband, can lay claim to the trouble following us. Sharing too many details right now would only put the women in more danger. However, we do need the jewelry Amber asked her mother about. It is vital to solving a case I've been working on."

Harold pushed a padded envelope across the counter. It bore the name Barbara Whitney, but no return address or postage. The package looked untouched. "Max came to see her about a month before he died, wanted to apologize for the past, and said he'd changed. She told him she hoped he really meant it, but still refused his gift of jewelry. He'd mailed it to her back in December. She sent it back. He decided to hand deliver the piece in person to convince her to keep it. Max gave her a ring. She wasn't about to take another one of those from the man. He told her to keep it because Amber was the creator. That's the only thing that kept her from throwing it in the trash."

"Thank you, Harold. It looks like Barbara is in good hands. I worked with Max for a while as an undercover bodyguard. I remember he took a solo vacation around that time, against my recommendation."

"What about our Amber? You two were looking mighty cozy when you got out of your vehicle a few minutes ago." Harold leaned his head to one side and seemed to be studying Graham.

"She is still feeling effects of the ether. I needed to support her." Graham swallowed.

"Are you sure that's all? Both of you looked a little star-struck to this old teacher."

The man's gaze made Graham uncomfortable. He needed to learn how to do the teacher look. He'd fallen victim to it too many times in the last few days.

Heat rose under his non-existent collar. Man, he needed to get a decent shirt, one that didn't reveal the color that was probably breaking out on his open neck above the tee shirt. Searching for a change of subject, he thought about their last interaction with the criminals. They now knew what Carlton's SUV looked like. It was time for a change. "Is there a rental place where I can get a different ride?"

Harold chuckled. "How about you give our girl her ginger ale, and then meet me out front to look at my truck. I've been thinking about trading it in. Maybe you could use it for a while and then come back here for a proper visit when this is all over."

"Sounds good. You wouldn't happen to have an old dress shirt you could loan me for a while? I'm getting a little tired of advertising my superhero status."

A squeal from the living room made both men run in that direction.

~~~~~

Graham rushed in with his sidearm drawn. "What's going on?"

Amber could not stop herself from grinning as she held Mom's left hand in the air. "Harold gave Mom an engagement ring today." She stood and gave her future stepfather a hug as she glared at Graham over her former teacher's shoulder. She hoped he'd put the gun away and settle down before he aggravated his wound. She watched as he stepped back into the kitchen and re-emerged without a drawn gun, holding her ginger ale.

"Congratulations, Harold and Barbara." He gave Amber her drink, and then shook the older couple's hands. His expression looked apologetic as he turned back and laid his palm across her wrist. Amber had trouble looking away from him until Harold spoke up.

"I invited Graham to check out my old truck. We were heading outside when we heard the commotion." He headed from the room, followed by Graham.

Amber snuggled into her mom's side. It had been a while since she'd visited, and it felt good to enjoy some time wrapped in her mother's love. She held the glass of ginger ale close and slowly sipped from the straw one of the men had thoughtfully included. Graham and Harold seemed to be hitting it off as they'd stepped from the room to talk trucks.

"Mom, when did you and Harold get so close?" Amber searched her mother's face, seeing a happier expression than she'd seen in years.

"We've only been serious for the last few months. He has always been there for us since we came here, but I was too afraid to acknowledge him as more than a friend. I figured I didn't know how to pick 'em because of marrying your father. I always wondered if it was something I did wrong and didn't want to make another bad decision."

Amber nodded in understanding. "I've kind of felt like men couldn't be trusted because of Dad. I never wanted any more contact with him after he deserted us. I pretty much succeeded in avoiding him until he hired me six months ago to make jewelry with his white stones. Now, every bad choice the man ever made has come blazing at me in the last few days. I think he was the one who chose evil over good, not us."

"I'm beginning to see that myself. A month before he died, your father
~~~~~

actually came here to apologize. That's when he insisted I take the jewelry. I didn't want it. I tried to give the piece back, but he said to keep the ring because you made it."

Leave it to Dad to lay a guilt trip on Mom. He may have come asking for forgiveness, but he still managed to manipulate those he once pretended to care about. His ploy kept the ring in the right hands, but also endangered them both. She forced a semi-pleasant response out through her lips. "Thanks for saving it. The jewelry will give us another clue into the mystery Dad left behind."

"I'm glad it will help. Max's visit allowed me to get over myself for thinking I was the problem. It made me realize I could finally open my heart to Harold, a good Christian man, who stood by me from the time we moved back here until today. I don't think I ever told you, but he and I had several dates in high school. Then I met your dad during college and thought I had found my forever husband."

"I'm sorry things didn't work out with you and Harold in the first place." Amber remembered when Harold had been her teacher and went out of the way to help struggling students. He'd been there for both of them all along. "Life would have been so different."

"I wouldn't have you, sweetheart. Other than knowing our Lord, you have been my reason for living. Harold is here for me now and that's all that matters. What about you and Graham? You two looked pretty chummy when you walked in. I saw the way he held onto your hand when he brought in the ginger ale. Your cheeks were as pink as the roses in my flower garden."

"I do admire the man. However, he seems unreachable right now. I've got my own trust issues with men, thanks to Dad. Maybe someday that will change. I must admit I've been tempted by the man's looks and personality. He was so patient with Jade." She paused and looked at her mom. "Were you aware that Dad had several other wives and a child after your marriage? His daughter Jade was born within a year after he left us."

Barbara sighed. "Max confessed to everything when he brought the jewelry to me. I didn't know about all the other relationships until then. Jade's mother was pregnant before our marriage ended. He'd been distant with me, but I didn't know why. He claimed the woman seduced him. We know he had a choice."

"Oh, Mom, I'm so sorry." Amber wondered how many of the other ex-wives were guilty of seduction, or had her father been the one opting to stray?

"At least the man tried to change at the end of his life. We can dwell on the past, or we can make our own changes, like getting engaged." Mom smiled as she glanced through a window toward the men standing outside.

The cell phone sitting next to her mother rang. She turned it over and looked at the identification. "It's your Uncle Warren. Would you like to speak to him?"

"Sure." Amber had always appreciated him giving her a start in making jewelry. He'd taken her under his wing when her father dumped them. The lapidary skills she had learned gave her the freedom to live the life she wanted.

Mom greeted her brother. "Hi, Warren. What's that? I'm fine, but I can't tell you where I'm at right now. Yes, she's here. I'll let you speak to her."

Amber held the cell to her ear. "Hey, Uncle Warren, it's good to hear from you."

"Hi, my favorite gemstone. Look, I'm all kinds of worried about you. There were some men here a few minutes ago looking for you and Barbara. I told them I thought you were up north and Barbara was probably at home."

The secure feeling that had washed over her from his familiar voice sank like the *Titanic* when he mentioned the visitors. "Did they hurt you?"

"No, they just wanted to know if I'd seen my sister or niece today. They left when I didn't provide any answers."

"They've been following me all over the country. Dad gave out jewelry I'd made. It has something to do with an FBI case. I've got my own special FBI agent who's taking care of me. What do you think of that?"

Silence filled the other end of the phone. Why didn't he answer?

"Are you okay, Uncle Warren? Did those guys come back?" She wanted to jump through space and rescue her uncle.

"No, but I think you and your special agent should stop by my place before you head out of town. I'm sorry." He paused.

"What do you know?" Her voice wavered. Could she trust any man?

"I'll explain when you get here. I have a feeling your FBI man planned on coming here, regardless of this conversation." He gave a hesitant good-bye and disconnected.

She hugged her mom. Frustration fought with anger as she pondered her uncle's evasive words. "Uncle Warren seems to be in on this puzzle. You stay safe here with Harold until we tell you otherwise. We need to get back on the road."

"Let me fix you some sandwiches. Give me a few more minutes to mother my daughter. While I find some snacks, would you like to borrow the shower in Harold's guest room? It's the first door on the left side of the hallway. My bag is in there. Help yourself to some fresh clothes if you like. I know they're not exactly your style and will fit loosely, but they're clean."

Amber looked down and noticed blood stains on her shirt for the first time. "That sounds wonderful, just what Dr. Mom ordered."

~~~~~

An hour later, Amber took in the view as Graham drove Harold's truck down the town's quaint Main Street lined with storefront businesses. Several stores sat empty with signs for leasing them. Amber sighed. She remembered a bustling downtown area with Warren's Jewelry at the heart of the place.

She fingered the floral top her mom loaned her. The faint scent of her mother's lavender toiletries filled her senses with a moment of calm before the storm. Her uncle seemed hesitant to talk over the phone. She wondered what that meant. Did his hesitancy spell more troubled waters in the future?

She might as well enjoy the scenery before they got there. Graham looked distinguished in one of Harold's plaid dress shirts. The sleeves were long enough to cover up his bandages and the blue and tan colors of the shirt highlighted his brown eyes. It didn't hurt that he had cleaned up well using Harold's pine-scented soap.

He hadn't asked for directions to the jewelry shop. Maybe Harold had told him how to get there while she showered. She liked Harold. He'd always been good to Mom and her. Now the older couple could finally have the relationship they deserved, one filled with trust.

"Harold must have given you good directions to Uncle Warren's."

"I already had them memorized from when your dad gave me the addresses."

"I totally forgot he was on your list, between our injuries and Mom and Harold's good news." Doubts roared like Daniel's hungry lions as she wondered what her uncle and Graham knew that she didn't. "I should have warned him when I called Mom. What if those men had harmed him?"

"He didn't fit the pattern of ex-wives. I figured he'd be safe since the crooks don't seem to realize what we're getting from each of your father's recipients."

"Uncle Warren would still fit as an ex-in-law. They figured out enough to go to his store looking for Mom and me." The thought of harm coming to her uncle seared through her chest. She crossed her arms and glared out the window as Graham slowed Harold's truck and expertly parallel-parked in front of the jewelry store. Seeing her uncle in the window of his shop sent a breath of relief through her chest. Hopefully there was one man she could trust.

She pushed her floppy hat onto her head and ran from the truck to the store. Her uncle welcomed her with a hug that spelled home. She glanced around at the familiar shop where her love of jewelry-making had emerged. "I see you still have your antique cash register. I found one almost like it for my shop."
~~~~~

"She's a beauty, all right, though she hasn't been used as much lately." Warren pulled a handkerchief from his pocket and swiped it across his broad forehead, a sure sign he'd been shaken up by the men who'd come looking for her.

Graham interrupted her thoughts. "We'd like to see the jewelry that Max sent you. There's something we need to retrieve from it and then be on our way."

"About that, I've got some explaining to do." Warren looked down and fiddled with a velvet sleeve filled with lapidary tools. "Shortly after Amber completed making the jewelry, Max approached me about adding a hidden space in each of them. He figured since you apprenticed under me, I'd be able to add the space without changing your design too much. I figured it was another one of his underhanded schemes and didn't want to get involved at first."

"Then why did you?" Amber's trust in men took a dive off a cliff, headed for sharp rocks.

"The jewelry business has gone downhill with the recent economic conditions. Max offered me more than enough money to ride out several years of ups and downs. He didn't tell me what it was about. I still don't really know. But, when he sent me the tie-tack you made, my curiosity got the best of me."

He pulled a small locked box from below his display case. "Guess this is what you are looking for." After unlocking it, he lifted the lid and revealed another diode. Amber snagged an eyepiece from the top of the glass display case and examined it. This one had a green stripe of paint and a faint S etched on the side.

Graham held out his hand for the diode.

Amber fisted the eyepiece. "I can't believe you and I both got sucked into Dad's scheme. If he gave you more money than he gave me, you can afford to lend me this magnifier. I might need it to figure out why we're going to all this trouble." She hesitated and grabbed the sleeve of tools. "I'll borrow these too." She spun around and marched toward the door, trying to keep tears of regret and anger from falling down her cheeks like a waterfall.

"I'm sorry, sweetheart." The sound of Uncle Warren's pleading voice followed her.

"I'm sorry too. I love you, Uncle Warren, but I need some time to process this." She hurried from the store and clicked the remote to the truck. She sank into the passenger's seat, with tears raining down her cheeks.

Chapter Ten

Graham thanked Amber's Uncle Warren, who looked like an army had marched over him, body and soul. "I'll be in touch when this case heads to court. We will need your testimony."

"Of course. Tell Amber I'm sorry." Warren's shoulders slumped.

"Give her time, but I can't promise you anything." Graham stepped from the shop and looked into the pickup truck. Amber's hands covered her bowed head until she swiped one hand across a cheek. Tears, he hated tears. His ex-fiancée had used them like a sword to cut down his resolve on any issue. When he wised up to her fake crying bouts, she'd turned to his brother for sympathy. Now he only had pity for his brother. His ex dropped his sibling like a hot skillet when the woman cooked up a romance with a man richer than either of them.

He climbed into Harold's truck but opted for avoidance when he thought about saying something to his sniffling passenger. He turned the key in the ignition and headed out of town on country roads. The enemy had run out of relatives to pick on, so hopefully they wouldn't be able to follow them to their next stop in Kentucky. Unless someone spotted them leaving town, they should be safe for a while. He had no idea what Max's relationship with the next man was. At this point, he didn't care. He wanted the case to end so he could get back to working with his team and away from the tempting woman sitting beside him, giving him the silent treatment.

As he pulled away from the curb, he checked the mirrors for traffic and for followers. A twinge of pain from his injured arm lasted only a moment. Barbara and Harold's hospitality and pain relief tablets had helped ease the discomfort. Traffic seemed sparse in the small town. He headed for the highway once more and entered the on-ramp, only to spot the familiar sedan pull out from behind a billboard near the highway entrance.

"I can't believe they found us again. This is unbelievable. Hang on."

From the corner of his eye, he saw Amber cringe and grab onto the passenger side armrest. He pushed the pedal down and was pleased with how quickly the vehicle accelerated to way above the speed limit. Harold had not been kidding when he'd bragged about the truck's power. The sedan held its own, drawing nearer. The car rammed into the back of the truck. Graham felt a sudden drag from the rear, slowing the truck.

He pushed the gas pedal harder. The truck roared but didn't move faster. "Something isn't right. Can you look back and see if you can tell what's going on?"

Amber swung to the side and pushed up high in her seat. She gasped. "You're not going to believe this. I think they hooked onto the truck's hitch. The driver has his hand up in the air, waving for us to pull over."

Graham growled. "Not if I can help it. Harold said this powerhouse would haul anything, not that he thought we'd need it." He started swerving from side to side. The sedan would either come loose, or both vehicles would be in a jackknifed wreck. Thank the Lord for the lack of traffic. At least no one else would be hurt from the fallout.

Metal screeched. Amber cried out. He prayed and swayed. Then the truck jerked forward, leaving the sedan sliding to the side of the road with puffs of steam coming from under the hood. He hoped they wouldn't try to follow.

Graham decided to use side roads until they reached the next major city. Amber stared at the passing countryside without saying a word about what had just happened.

By the time they reached Cincinnati, Amber's head had fallen to the side. Deep breathing indicated she would at least get a little peace while sleeping. He wove through city streets and crossed the Ohio River on the suspension bridge instead of the highway. A long barge steamed its way under the bridge, sitting low in the wide, muddy river. The bright blue bridge stood out in contrast to gray clouds gathering in the sky. A bold sign welcomed them to Kentucky.

He checked all the mirrors. No one seemed to be following. He went up the ramp to Interstate 75 and headed for the hills, literally. The next address would take them to a mountain town in the eastern part of Kentucky.

He had no idea who Rupert Lee, care of *Lee's Wilderness Adventures and Cabins*, might be. When he'd mentioned the name to Amber, she had not recognized the man. They could go in as tourists and possibly catch a glimpse of the man at work before they asked about the jewelry. When he'd studied a map to memorize the route to the place, it had been several miles off of 25E near the edge of a mountain range.

If traffic flowed, they'd be there by evening. Renting a cabin might be a good idea. Hopefully one with two bedrooms, since Amber still stewed and deserved her privacy. Rain spattered the windshield. He focused on driving through the storm, which despite turning into a downpour, was much more relaxing than worrying about Amber and the rest of their journey.

~~~~~

Rain gave way to foggy clouds, as hills gave way to mountains. When
~~~~~

Graham slowed to turn off at Corbin, Kentucky, Amber finally looked his way. Other than puffy bags below her eyes, she seemed calm. He waited for her to speak.

Graham had noticed her waking up an hour ago, but she'd focused on the scenery since then. A few spring blossoms still splashed their color across dense green forests as their elevation rose with each twist in the road. Corbin's bright signs for every type of restaurant, including the chicken that put Kentucky on the map, interrupted the vista of forested mountains as they made their way onto 25E.

Amber sighed, a deep heaving one, and stretched. "I've always wanted to say I've eaten at the Colonel's original restaurant."

Tension dropped from Graham's shoulders. "Then let's take a slight detour to the south and get something to eat." He took a right at the next intersection. Moments later, he parked the truck in an empty space next to a pair of antique gas pumps near the former gas station turned chicken restaurant.

Soon, meaty juices covered their fingers as they savored the original spices. The food seemed to bolster both their moods. They took a few minutes to enjoy the displays of memorabilia in the museum side of the venue before returning to the road. The restaurant had gone from a struggling gas station, with few customers, to a booming international restaurant that literally fought off the competition in the early days.

"The Colonel was quite an entrepreneur. I just hope my art studio will take off and fly easier than his first efforts." Amber smiled for the first time since she'd left her mother's side.

"The important thing to learn is that he kept trying no matter what happened. The Colonel was flexible enough to know when to partner up with someone who could help when the restaurant grew into something too big for him to handle alone." Graham hoped he'd be able to get some of his fellow agents partnered up with them soon. His body screamed for a break from lack of sleep.

Graham's mind wandered to a little-known fact about the restaurant that he'd learned from watching a History Channel show. "Did you know the Colonel had a shoot-out with an early competitor? The displays in the restaurant didn't mention the event, but the other man started the fight. Sanders ended it by answering fire. The fact that he wounded the man didn't help Colonel Sanders gain popularity, even though it was self-defense." Graham thought of his wounded arm and grimaced.

She looked directly at Graham. Her innocent green eyes widened as she rubbed her arm. It looked like a bruise had developed from one of the encounters with the men trying to kidnap her.

"Have you ever had to kill anyone?"

"Not yet. I have injured someone, like the Colonel did. The trauma from that action can be devastating if you dwell on it too much. Most law enforcement personnel get some time off and counseling after an incident." He touched his injured arm and stifled a groan.

"Will the FBI want you to take time off for your arm?" She frowned.

Had he reacted to the pain out loud? He placed both hands on the steering wheel and forced a neutral expression onto his face. "They might if I let my supervisor know. I'm doing fine except for some minor pain."

"You can play the tough guy role, but I may need some serious counseling before this journey is over." Amber sighed. "To which of my father's unknown to me acquaintances are we headed for now? We're out of ex-wives and relatives except for Great-Uncle Jethro. You said we'd see him last. Should we warn him they might be coming?"

"I'll communicate with him later tonight." He should have taken care of that before things started escalating.

"How about we both do the communicating?" Amber crossed her arms and frowned. "I sure hope your FBI buddy is taking good care of Jade."

"She's in good hands. Jade would have enjoyed going to our next destination. Rupert Lee is the owner of a wilderness adventure business. I don't know what relationship the man had with Max, other than being a recipient of your jewelry." Graham focused on the hazy mountains and the increasing curves in the road.

"I never heard of Rupert before starting this journey, so I can't help you. As long as we aren't headed toward another showdown with guns, I'll survive." She wrapped her arms around her body and slumped in her seat.

"I agree. Hey, is that a bear over there?" He slowed and watched a medium-sized bear lumber into the woods.

"Too bad I don't have my phone to take a picture." She leaned forward for a better look.

"Not a good idea, even if you did have your phone on. We probably still smell enough like Kentucky's best fried chicken to ensure the bear would rip Harold's truck to pieces for a bite." When she shuddered, he asked, "You do know what to do if you meet a bear, don't you?"

"Maybe run like crazy or tell him Yogi already took my picnic basket?" Her tinkling laughter tempted Graham to join her, but bears were a serious threat.

"That's the last thing you want to do. He'd enjoy the chase. You want to make yourself look as big as you can and make a bunch of noise to scare him off."

"And pray he doesn't like people food, or should I say people for food." Amber clapped her hands together, cocking her head to the side. Graham decided she must be really nervous if her jokes were any indication.

"Right. Keep watching. You might spot some other interesting wildlife." He hoped she'd spot a less exciting distraction.

Several deer and groundhogs later, they neared the turn-off for the road that would lead them to *Lee's*. The sun broke through the cloudy skies and cast its last shadowed rays across tall pine trees when they finally entered the parking lot for *Lee's Wilderness Adventures and Cabins*.

The gum-smacking guy in the rental office leased them a two-bedroom cabin for the night, and told them his boss, Rupert Lee, would be there first thing in the morning. Dark shadows covered the cabin as they pulled in front and shut off the truck's lights. They both jumped when a shadowed shape sprinted across the porch.

Chapter Eleven

The next morning, Amber sat in front of the cabin's large screened window. She was glad that their scare last night had only been a raccoon racing across the cabin porch. The Bible Graham had purchased for her lay open to the 121st Psalm. She'd needed the passage's comforting words about looking up into the hills for help. The mountains pictured through her window frame were a comforting reaffirmation of the scripture. She filled her lungs with the fresh morning air filtering through the open window's screen. Cardinals twittered and flew around a birdbath sitting near the cabin.

For the first time since meeting Graham, her mind turned to jewelry making. An enameled bird sprinkled with tiny gemstones might make a perfect addition to her creations for the art store. Her fingers itched to create the design. She thanked her Creator for the inspiration. A notepad and pen sat on a side table. She filled the rest of her quiet time by doodling out a possible pin or necklace featuring either a blue jay or a cardinal. It might even fit well on a metal bookmark. She became so lost in her designs that she jumped when Graham leaned over her shoulder. His warm breath brushed her ear.

"Those look nice. Are they going to be pieces for your studio sales?" His mint-scented breath warmed the side of her face. Confused thoughts swirled in her mind.

"I think so. If I get home in one piece, these little birds will make a great line of jewelry. It feels good to do something creative this morning. The activity helps me forget what happened with my Dad and the jewelry."

"What about Warren? Do you think you can forgive him?" He stepped away and she was able to think straight.

"As a Christian, I will forgive my much-loved uncle. Dad used us both. However, true forgiveness may take me a few days to get over Uncle Warren falling for my father's scheme. I wish he'd contacted me or the authorities when he discovered the diode or after the funeral."

"Maybe your dad scared him into silence. We're dealing with some really bad guys and Warren doesn't look like he could take on the ones we've seen."

"That is true. I guess in the long run, it's good he still has his store. I practically lived at Uncle Warren's after we moved there. Mom kept busy teaching, and he taught me how to make jewelry."

The sound of a loud engine interrupted their conversation. They ran to the front door. The gum-chewing guy who registered them the night before waved from his beefed-up car to an older man standing on the porch of the office.

"Let's go meet Mr. Rupert Lee and see if he kept the jewelry Max sent him." Graham held the screen door open for their exit.

Warm morning sunshine greeted Amber as she and Graham left their cabin and strolled down the short path toward the rental office.

"Howdy, folks, did you have a good rest here at my wilderness adventure?" A bald man greeted them as they approached. An unbuttoned plaid shirt barely covered the *Lee's Adventures* tee shirt underneath.

"We did. Are you Rupert?" Graham shook the man's hand.

"I am. We have several adventures for explorers of all levels. Would you be interested in something easy or more challenging?" Rupert pulled a brochure from his shirt pocket and held it out.

Amber accepted the paper without looking at it. "Actually, we're here on a different kind of challenge. One my father, Max Whitney, forced us to accept."

"Ah, good old Max, he did like to set up mysteries for people to solve. I hadn't heard much from him since college, and then around Christmas he sent me a key chain with a white rock on it. He told me to hang on to it until he could come for a visit and reveal something special about it." He waved them over to a circle of Adirondack chairs.

Amber took the chair he offered and leaned forward in anticipation. "We need to look at that key chain."

"So Max has hidden a clue to your mystery on it somewhere?" Rupert leaned back in the chair and wrapped his arms around his plump belly.

Graham stiffened in the chair next to Amber. "How did you know?"

Rupert chuckled. "It was a game he often played with our group of college companions. He would organize these scavenger hunts with complicated layers we had to figure out. Most of us didn't get far with them. I hope you do better with your challenge. How is Max doing these days?"

"Unfortunately, he passed away," Graham answered before Amber could.

She was thankful he'd replied. Anger still warred with proper grief. Somewhere in the back of her memory she recalled her father setting up scavenger hunts for her to follow. When she didn't understand the clues, he'd made her feel dumb for not knowing the answers. She'd shoved those memories so far back that it had been years since they'd come to the surface.

"I'm sorry to hear about his death. He could be a prankster, but you must miss Max. He was a good friend to me during college, very competitive, but always did the right thing in the end." Rupert looked up as a falcon floated overhead on broad wings. "Since he's gone, you'll have to figure out the answers on your own without his help. Good luck with that. Max had quite a mind for creating mysteries to solve."

"Can we see the key chain? We'd like to collect our clue and get on our way." Amber didn't want to hear any more praise for her father.

"Unfortunately, I don't have it today."

A frown formed on Graham's face. Amber could only imagine the contortions revealed in her own expression.

"No worries, you two. My daughter has the keychain and will be back in about four days. I keep the keys to our supply sheds on that ring. We have several huts located strategically in the hills. She's leading a group of people on one of our adventures right now and will get food and camping gear from the sheds as needed."

Graham's knee bounced. "Is there a way to meet up with her sooner?"

"She's about a day ahead of you, but with the group of rookies she took out yesterday, they probably haven't gotten too far up the trail. If you hustle you could probably reach them by nightfall, and then get back here tomorrow afternoon."

"I don't think we're exactly prepared to take on a mountain." Amber looked down at her odd selection of clothing and her mesh athletic shoes.

"No problem. I can sell or rent everything you need. I even have a pretty good selection of hiking boots." The salesmanship in the man's expression gleamed.

Definitely a friend of her father's when it came to making a profit. Amber looked away, fighting the urge to speak her thoughts out loud.

"Our trails are well marked. You'll have a good time. Maybe you two will decide to join the group and finish out the tour, after reaching my Christy." Rupert pointed the way to his camp store.

~~~~~

An hour later, they'd left their cabin and started the uphill trek. Humidity from the previous day's rain filled the air and dampened the slick trail, making them slow down to take cautious steps. Amber paused for a breath.

"I can't believe that man suckered us into buying all this gear for one night on the mountain. You used up a chunk of your friend Carlton's cash. I hope you can get a refund from the FBI when this is all over."

"I've been considering doing some hiking. This purchase may be the tipping point for forcing me to make that decision." He gazed up the trail. "It looks like we're headed for a walk in the clouds."

"If you ask me, we've been lost in a fog for the last few days." Amber
~~~~~

forced her feet to move and headed up the misty trail.

"Are you getting stressed again?"

Graham's chortle made her want to throttle the man, who seemed to be climbing without any shortness of breath. He even had the lung power to laugh at her inane idiom.

"You could say that. My legs feel like wet noodles. Both lungs are on fire. And now I can barely see two feet in front of me." As if to emphasize their condition, she managed to stumble over a root in the trail and fall to her knees. "I wish I'd gotten those hiking poles Rupert had at his store. I need one for both my North and South Pole."

"I saw you admiring the trekking poles. I went back in while you were changing clothes. This is your lucky day." He set his backpack down and pulled out the extendable walking sticks and delivered them to her. Then he placed a hand under each of her armpits and hoisted her to a standing position.

"Thanks, I think. Maybe I should share one with you so I don't have to pick you up off of the ground." The poles would help with balance, but she doubted they'd solve her breathing issue.

Graham grinned and pulled a matching set of poles out for his use. "I came prepared."

"Well, aren't you the Boy Scout." She lifted her poles and started making her way up the cloud-covered trail.

"Right now, I'm scouting for snakes. Thump your walking sticks along the ground as we move forward. If we make enough noise, chances are the critters will clear the path before we even see them in this dense fog."

Amber stopped in her tracks and waved him ahead. "You can take the lead. I'll let you spot any serpents first. I know how to use self-defense, but I'm pure chicken when it comes to snakes." A chill ran down her spine.

"Just let me know if I'm setting too fast a pace." Graham's steps slowed as he looked at her over his shoulder.

"I'm right behind you." Amber pushed herself to keep as close as she could without running over him. She did not like snakes.

The thick cloud surrounded them. The sound of their moving feet and thumping sticks seemed contained in a bubble of moisture. It could have been her imagination, but she found it suddenly easier to breathe. She looked around and admired the budding trees and mossy patches at the bottom of their trunks. Her thoughts moved away from snakes to the wonder of God's beautiful world. *Thump.* She bumped into Graham's back.

"Don't move a muscle. I'm seeing something ahead on the trail." His whisper filled her with angst.

"Are you just trying to scare me?"

"No, now be quiet and stay behind me."

Amber peered around Graham's side and saw the coiled serpent ahead, waving a menacing tail in the air. *Help us, Lord, make it go away.* She prayed harder than she had in the last few days. She held on to Graham's backpack and waited until he lifted his pole and gave a loud thump. Underbrush whispered with the sound of the snake moving on.

For the next few hours their progress was slow and steady until at last the sun broke through the clouds. Amber looked back down the trail. A sense of wonder filled her. "It's beautiful. I feel like we are sitting in a mansion up in the clouds. My mom used to sing about a mansion over the hilltop. I wonder if the songwriter saw what we're seeing now."

The clouds all sat below where they stood, surrounding the mountain like a halo. Her earthly father had left a mess for her to figure out, but her Heavenly Father always came through in the long run.

The song about a heavenly mansion ran across her mind and out through her lips as she tried to sing the song under her puffing breath. Graham hummed along, creating a sweet harmony. For a while the trail leveled out, and the companions belted out several praise songs. They stopped near a trickling stream and enjoyed jerky, cheese, and dried fruit for lunch. Amber and Graham sealed their trash in plastic and resumed their trek in silence as the path grew steeper and the hours passed.

Graham stopped and pointed to the sky. Two eagles circled above their heads. Their dark shapes glided across the early evening sky. Splashes of pink, yellow, and orange softened the western horizon.

He broke their silence with a quiet voice. "Look for a huge nest in a tree. They might have a family near here."

Amber spun in a circle and squinted as she studied a tree silhouetted against the bright multicolored sky. "I think I see a nest." Her voice fell to a whisper as she gazed up at a collection of sticks spanning at least five feet between branches. The eagles swooped closer and landed on the nest. She watched in awe until loud voices sounded from above their location.

"I think we may be getting close to our adventurers." Graham started walking toward the sound.

"Yeah, it sounds like they are shouting at the top of their lungs. I wonder if something is wrong."

"I've only been on one other hiking trip, but I don't recall having a group scream fest as part of getting to know nature better." Graham's gaze shifted to take in the scenery like he was searching for something.

A loud voice rang out from above where they stood. This time the words were clear.

"Go away, bear!"

Heavy pounding rumbled down the trail, coming nearer and nearer.

"Bear? Should we scream?" Amber's voice shook. She fought back the urge to panic.

"Not this time, unless we want the beast to head back up the trail toward the other group." Graham pulled Amber from the path and held her close to his chest. "For now, we'll sit tight and hope the bear doesn't want to mess with us."

His breath was warm against her ear as he held her. Shivers of both fear and emotions she couldn't deal with right now sent shafts of ice through her veins. *Please, God, spare us from this bear.* The bear's thudding feet came closer. Graham's arms tightened as the bear stopped and sniffed the air near where they stood. A musky scent made its way into Amber's nose. Another round of screams sounded from the other group. The bear let out a growl and meandered farther down the trail, making loud noises of its own. Amber started shaking uncontrollably.

Graham held her closer. "Are you going to be all right?"

Her shaking turned into laughter and tears. Hysterics had never been part of her personality. There was always a first time for everything.

"He's gone, sweetheart." He leaned in closer.

Calm swept over her like a gentle waterfall.

Her mind turned away from the bear, even though the beast bellowed like a sick cow. Right now, she felt sure she was making cow-eyes at the man as he held her face with his hands and leaned his forehead against hers. Where had her resolve to resist Graham's obvious charm gone? She pushed away and shivered like she'd lost a blanket's warmth.

"I'll be okay. I just thought a bear growl might sound mightier than a lonely cow's mooing." Uncontrolled giggling erupted from her lips.

Graham looked puzzled, then he chuckled. "I'm glad you haven't lost your sense of humor."

"If you recall, I tend to find it at the worst of times." She heaved out a large breath and adjusted her backpack straps.

"Speaking of bad times, let's see if we can catch the others. We might want to make some people noise so they don't think the bear is coming back." Graham turned his back on Amber. The evening took on a chill.

Chapter Twelve

Graham couldn't believe he'd called her sweetheart. The terminology brought back some seriously bad connections. His ex-fiancée overused the endearment on him, and later on his brother, to the point the word lost its meaning. Hopefully, Amber hadn't taken his comment seriously. In his mind he'd really believed she was a sweetheart when the word escaped, but now he wanted to run up the mountain and hide in case she actually heard him.

"Hello, campers, we're trying to catch up to you." Amber's voice rang out from behind him. He echoed her sentiments, and before long they reached the other hikers.

"Did you see the bear?" An elementary-aged boy danced around his parents and a teen girl who looked to still be recovering from the sighting.

Another couple wearing matching backpacks stood to the side holding hands.

An athletic redhead looked at them curiously. Her arms were crossed. "You should realize this mountain is private property and for use only by patrons of *Lee's Adventures.*"

"You must be Christy Lee. Your father, Rupert, gave us permission to catch up with you." Graham offered his hand. She uncrossed her arms but didn't reach toward his.

"Do you have papers to give me verifying that you signed our waivers?" This time her hand reached out, but the palm faced up.

Graham smiled and winked at the woman. He didn't try to use his good looks often, but sometimes it worked to his advantage. "Rupert gave us special permission to travel here on our own. We were in a hurry. I'm sorry he forgot to give us the papers. Your dad thought you would be the one who could solve a major mystery for us."

The woman's stance softened some, but she still insisted they needed to have the appropriate paperwork. A slight smile crossed her face as she looked him up and down. Amber coughed beside him.

When Graham looked at Amber, she held a hand over a half-hidden smirk and shook her head before facing the woman. "Look, Miss Lee, this grinning goofball is from the FBI, and my father is Max Whitney. Max sent your father a key ring that I made for him. We need to examine it and see if it has something in it we can remove."

"FBI, huh? I've got some orange groves in Alaska for you to look at."

She waved her party of adventurers farther up the trail.

Graham held out his badge. Christy took a look. "I guess I can give you the benefit of the doubt if you can describe the key chain."

Amber took a step closer to the woman. "The piece is made of a polished white quartz stone in a setting of swirled silver. The clip for holding keys is also silver-toned."

Christy pulled it from her backpack and removed the key clip from the stone setting. "You can look at the stone. I'll hang on to my keys since they mean the difference between starvation and feasting for my hikers."

Graham looked over Amber's shoulder as she laid out the tools from her Uncle Warren's shop and operated on the key chain. She carefully pulled back the bent silver wires gripping the stone. Just like the other pieces, there was a thin band of gold around the stone.

This time it was white gold, but the catch to open the stone and reveal the diode worked the same. Before she finished putting the piece back together, Graham had unpacked a newly purchased flashlight from his pack. He held it over her shoulder, providing extra light as Amber completed her work.

Christy watched for a while and then left to help the hiking group put up small tents for the night. The redhead sent a smile his way and offered to set up their tents also. Graham thanked her, but refused the offer when he heard Amber huff. He was in big trouble. One woman paid him attention, and the other seemed to be drawing a circle around herself as she tried to solve her father's mystery. He suspected Amber had heard him say sweetheart and then watched the attempted flirting with the guide, to get what they needed.

~~~~~

Graham and Amber erected their tents in relative silence. She sighed out a "goodnight" after pounding in her last peg. She pressed her gear through the door and crawled inside, saying she was exhausted.

He sat and watched the last glowing embers die away in the campfire where the group had roasted marshmallows earlier. Christy had offered them each one of the gooey snacks during the fellowship with the other hikers. Amber refused the treat, saying she didn't need sticky fingers. Graham ate both, but somehow the s'mores hadn't tasted as sweet as he thought they might.

Graham looked up, amazed at how many stars filled the clear night. With no streetlights to dim his view, he could see traces of what might be the Milky Way.

"The sky is beautiful tonight." Christy's voice came from behind him.

He needed to straighten things out before they went any farther. "Look, I need to level with you. I only flirted in hopes of getting the information we needed."
~~~~~

"No worries, I figured out real quick who you were actually interested in. She seems like a nice woman, other than the cold shoulder she's turned my way since you plastered your goofy smile on your face and flapped your eyelashes at me. I hope she realizes how much you really love her."

"She's an assignment. This will be over in a few days and we'll go our separate ways." At least, that was what he kept telling himself.

"Whatever you say, Mister, thanks for confirming the old adage that love is blind. You better go ahead and turn in. The trail down will be easier, but after today's climb, your muscles will let you know otherwise." Christy kicked dirt over the campfire and headed for her tent.

Graham took one more look at the stars. Could Christy be right? Was he falling for Amber? He shook his head and rose from where he had been sitting for over an hour. The woman was wrong. Amber would be out of his life soon. He had no plans to pursue a relationship, ever. Christy was right about one thing. His muscles were stiffening up already.

~~~~~

The next morning, Amber crawled from her tent and limped to where he leaned against his loaded backpack. He held out a granola bar, which she stuffed in her mouth without saying a word. She stiffly thanked Christy for helping them and refused his help as she packed up her gear. Good, she kept her distance. He should be happy, but a big part of him missed hearing her voice.

He turned away from watching her and looked down the mountain. Clear skies revealed a glory-filled dawn. He prayed for strength to make it through the rest of their journey without mishap from either the criminals or the condition of his bachelor's heart. Getting involved with Amber was not part of the assignment. Though, she sure was an interesting person.

The tap of hiking poles and hesitant feet coming closer made him turn around and take in another beautiful view. Humidity had curled the waves in her shoulder-length hair. The temptation to feel its texture was strong. Instead, he nodded and turned back down the trail.

"We should have a pretty easy descent."

"If you say so, just watch out for the snakes and bears." Her words sounded clipped, like she was in pain or angry or jealous. Had Christy been right about the two of them? He didn't want to think about the possibility, though it made something in his masculine heart give a jolt. He hurt on both the inside and out. Surely she must be in pain too.

"Are you feeling all right?" Dumb question, considering how much his muscles were protesting this morning.

"I'm fine." Her flat voice said she was anything but fine.

Maybe he should just keep his mouth shut and focus on getting them
~~~~~

safely off the mountain. They did need to make some noise in case the bear decided to cross their path again. He thought about the songs they'd sung together yesterday and started singing praise choruses. It took a while, but she eventually joined in, just not as jubilantly as before. She was definitely hurting, but he wasn't about to ask about being all right again.

"Let me know if you need to take a break." His words gave her the power to decide about her pain level.

"I'd rather just get this over with." At least she was talking.

"Sure." He upped their rate of speed and went back to singing. When the trail leveled out they made even better time. They'd be back where they started by early afternoon if they could keep the same tempo down the last part of the incline. He pushed even harder as the trail headed downwards and she kept up.

"Ouch, ugh." Amber's cries rang out as loose stones flew into Graham's back. One of her hiking boots connected with his calf, throwing him off balance. He staggered. Amber hit the ground with a thud. She groaned and wrapped her hands around her ankle. Tears streamed down her cheeks. She lifted a hand to wipe the tears away.

"Freeze."

"Is it a snake?"

"No, you landed in a patch of poison ivy. If you rub your face, you'll regret it."

"Great, I haven't had a case since I went to camp in junior high. I got a shot at the hospital when that happened. Most people wait several days before they react. My welts started showing the same day." She used her shoulder to wipe the tears away. Her eyes widened as she looked up in fear. "I carried an antihistamine with me for years. Since I don't use a purse anymore, I never thought about having those pills with me."

"Then we need to head down the trail and back to civilization before you start reacting." Graham helped her stand. She whimpered when she placed weight on her ankle. "It looks like we might need to get your ankle checked out too. Lean on me while I rearrange these backpacks."

Since they'd only packed for one night, he was able to stuff the contents from her bag into his, leaving her with an empty pack on her back. In the process he found a packet of wipes, and she cleaned her exposed skin as best she could and patted down her clothing.

He offered her his arm without the bullet wound and they slowly limped down the mountain. Long shadows covered Harold's truck by the time they reached *Lee's Adventures*. They'd left the vehicle packed with their few belongings. Graham threw their purchased gear in the back and helped Amber climb into the passenger seat.

She grabbed his hand before he could leave her side. "Thank you. I'm sorry I was cross with you this morning. I couldn't believe how you acted toward Christy. I felt like you were using her by flirting to get the information."

"I'm also sorry I pretended with her. She saw right through me, though. Sometimes in my job you have to do something you don't like in order to get what you need."

"I understand. I just didn't like it." Amber pulled the seatbelt across her lap and latched it in place.

"I'm sorry you have to go through this. The sooner we get this mystery solved, the happier we'll all be."

"Yeah, thanks a lot, Dad." She looked down at her arm where welts had formed during the remainder of their hike. "I don't like going to the doctor either, but I guess it's time for me to do something I don't like."

Graham's heart sank, seeing where her skin had broken out in pink blotches. He'd seen another person react to an allergen during a mission several years ago. It hadn't turned out well.

Chapter Thirteen

By the time they reached a small regional hospital, an hour away from the camp, welts covered Amber's palms and arms. Her ankle throbbed inside the tight boot. Graham suggested she keep the footwear on, reducing the swelling. Now, she wondered if the boot would ever come off. When the receptionist took note of Amber's high sensitivity to poison ivy, she'd made a call moving them up the priority list.

Graham guided the wheelchair he'd commandeered for Amber through the inner doors of the Emergency Room. She bowed her head and recalled the recent conversation. Hospital personnel hadn't questioned their relationship. Graham's presence was a comfort.

Moments after they entered a curtained room, a nurse scurried in. She confirmed Amber's name and birthday and read through a list of possible allergies and conditions. The nurse tapped Amber's answers into her tablet and took her vitals.

"The doctor should be in shortly. We'll take good care of you. Would you like help getting that boot off?"

"Yes, please." Amber moved to the bed and stretched her foot out in front. The woman loosened the laces and managed to wriggle it off without causing more than a moan to escape from her patient's lips. The nurse closed the curtain and made her exit.

A few minutes later, the curtains reopened with a swish. "Good evening, ma'am." A young doctor scanned the electronic chart in his hand. "Will you please confirm your name and birth date for me?"

Amber complied. The physician peered at her poison ivy without touching her hands and then used his gloved fingers to prod her ankle from every angle. She drew in a sharp breath and bit her lip.

"I think we may be looking at a sprained ankle, but we'll have radiology check it out. The nurse will get you started on an IV for the poison ivy reaction immediately. Is the rash only on your arms and hands?"

"For now. We patted down my clothing and skin with wipes so hopefully that took care of the oil."

"Good, but I'd suggest changing into something else as soon as possible. We'll give you a couple of hours for the IV to put an antihistamine into your system. If all goes well with radiology, we'll get you on your way. I don't recommend driving for a while, you'll be sleepy."

Radiology wheeled her away after the doctor left. A half-hour later, she had returned to the exam room, then the nurse stopped in and wrapped her ankle, confirming that it was only sprained. Amber settled in for a nap as her eyelids grew heavy from the drug in her system. She was vaguely aware of the low sound of a local television show in the background. Sometime later, Graham shook her shoulder. An older woman pushing a computer on wheels stood beside him.

"Hi, honey, I'm Rose from registration. We got your name at the front desk, but I need the rest of your data and insurance information."

"Sure, my cards are in the wallet behind my phone." Amber looked at Graham, who pulled her device from his pocket and handed it to her. She pulled out the cards and gave them to the woman.

Amber grinned at Graham as she stuffed her phone into her own pocket. He looked at the ceiling and shook his head. Rose scanned the cards and typed a few more words into her computer. The quiet droning from the local talk show stopped as a breaking news announcement blared. Rose looked up and frowned. Her face blanched. She leaned against the wheeled stand and started edging out of the room.

"Are you all right, Rose?" Graham stood and walked toward the woman, who let out a squeak and fled the room, leaving her computer behind.

"What in the world?" Amber glanced at the television where words on the screen proclaimed in large letters that a man claiming to be from the FBI was actually a dangerous criminal who was holding a woman hostage. Pictures of Graham and Amber filled the rest of the screen.

Graham stood and reached for their belongings. "It looks like our mole is trying to find out where we are. It's been quiet the last few days so he must have lost our trail. The phone number listed is definitely not FBI, but the photo reflects the one on my current ID."

Amber sat up. Drowsiness threatened, but she managed to gather her boot in one arm while Graham removed the IV from her other and wrapped her arm in gauze. She was relieved to see that the IV bag was nearly empty. Graham grabbed her insurance and identification cards from where the woman had left them and stuffed them into his pocket.

He wrapped his good arm around her waist and they hobbled through the nearby emergency room door for ambulance use. A muffled code announcement sounded from the building as they hurried from the hospital to where he had parked the truck. When Graham stepped away after helping her into the front seat, Amber felt a loss. She forced her muddled mind to make her hands function enough to drop her boot to the floor, fasten the seatbelt, and put pressure on where the IV had been in her arm. Graham put the vehicle in gear and pulled away from the parking lot without any lights shining from the truck. As they drove away, a security guard waving a gun appeared in her side mirror. She watched as the lone man quit running and leaned over like he was trying to catch his breath.

"I always wondered if there would be a wanted poster for my dad. I guess that honor is mine." Amber groaned at her attempt to lighten the mood.

Graham chuckled. "Don't take it to heart. That bulletin is as phony as baloney."

"I like bologna." Amber yawned and fought to stay awake but couldn't. Dreams of kissing Graham and fighting off villains dressed in bologna-covered ski masks invaded her coma-like state, followed by nothingness, until the rising sun burned through her eyelids.

~~~~

"Good morning, Sunshine." Graham's voice cut through the fog inside her brain.

"Hey, Graham." She stretched and looked at his profile. She'd had some interesting dreams, but that was over. Heat rushed to her cheeks. Amber turned her gaze toward the windshield, taking in a view of rolling hills and mountains in the distance. "Are we still in Kentucky?"

"It's definitely not Kansas anymore." Graham flashed his grin full of perfect teeth in her direction and chuckled.

"Ha ha, now who's being funny?" She tried to keep a straight face but couldn't.

Graham frowned. "I only drove about an hour away before I found this overlook. I thought it might be a good idea to stop. I contacted my boss and let him know about the fake bulletin while you rested. I also needed to catch a few winks of my own before things get worse."

"You certainly are the pessimist this morning." She looked across the vista and saw the wonders God had made for their viewing pleasure. Words of praise filtered into her thoughts until Graham interrupted.

"After last night, I'd say we have plenty to worry about." Graham tapped his fingers on the steering wheel. Amber watched as he tensed when a car passed their parking spot. His shoulders relaxed when the car kept going.

"That was quite a scare. I hope Rose didn't have a heart attack thinking we were the bad guys. How do you think the mole is doing all this?" Worries about misled law enforcement taking her from Graham's protection and handing her over to the kidnappers raced through Amber's thoughts.

"I don't know. Somehow they keep finding us. Whatever they were using must not have worked in the mountains so they resorted to the news bulletin. I didn't see any surveillance cameras in the hospital lot. I doubt they have much call for that kind of equipment in such a small village.
~~~~

Without surveillance, they wouldn't know which direction I took. The biggest problem will be if the false bulletin is shared on social media or radio and national television."

"I suppose we'll get our five minutes of unwanted fame." A wave of panic pushed down on her stomach. Would the mole's manipulation of the truth ruin all the hard work she'd put into starting her new business?

"Yeah, having my face broadcast everywhere will have an effect on any future undercover status for me." Graham rubbed his hand across his bristly chin.

He was long past a five o'clock shadow, but it looked good on the man. Another day and he wouldn't resemble the photograph on the TV. Who was she kidding? She'd recognize his handsome features anywhere. Amber shook her head and blamed any admiration on the drugs. This was the man who would use those handsome looks on a woman, like mountain climber Christy, by flirting with her to get what he wanted.

The pain creeping back into her arms, hands, and ankle distracted her from her irritation at the man. The welts had gone down some. The bruise from the attacker in her shop looked almost inflamed. Strange. "I don't suppose we'd be able to stop by a store and collect some antihistamine or antibiotic cream? I'd also like some water, so I can take some of those over-the-counter pain pills we got for your arm."

"That might be a good idea. If we spot another big-box store, we'll grab more snacks and whatever you need for your pain. We should probably check out the television section and see if we made the morning news." Graham started pulling his seatbelt back into place when the satellite phone rang. Their gazes met.

Graham picked up the phone and answered it. A frown creased his brow. A shard of fear stabbed at Amber's already stressed heart.

Chapter Fourteen

"Hey Carlton, what's up?" Graham's jaw dropped as he ran his hand through his thick head of hair. "Are you kidding me?"

"Is Jade all right?" Amber leaned closer, wondering what was going on. She hadn't seen Graham look that upset since their journey began.

"I'm putting the phone on speaker so Amber can hear you. Yeah, I think she needs to know all the facts." Graham pulled the phone back and pushed the speaker button.

Carlton's voice echoed across the truck cab. "My sister's boyfriend, Martin Johnson, took Jade. The good thing is that we now know the name of the mole. The bad thing is he has a hostage that he can use against you."

Amber gasped. She'd only known her sister for a day or two. It wasn't right to threaten the child. "This is terrible. She's a pretty strong-willed kiddo though." At least she hoped so. Amber slouched back against the seat. Her hands shook as they rested against her mouth in a prayer position. Could things get any worse?

"How much does she know about your mission?" Carlton's voice took on a demanding tone.

"She knows what we're looking for. I don't think she knew where we were going, but I can't guarantee anything." Graham shook his head.

"Is he going to be able to pump her for information?" Amber thought back to Julia's attack. The criminals would have a tough time breaking her sister, which would put Jade in harm's way.

"She's a smart girl, but it sounds like Martin had no problem wrapping Tamera around his proverbial finger. Who knows what he might succeed doing with a child." Graham pounded the steering wheel. Amber jumped, then laid a hand over his.

Carlton spoke up. "Hey, don't put it all off on Tamera. Martin knew you were working the case. The creep figured since you and I were best friends he could sweet talk my sister into sharing information she might overhear us talking about. The more he learned about Jade, the more he must have considered my sister a negotiable part of getting the information he needs."

"How could you let this happen? We left her in your care. You were supposed to watch her." Graham's voice rose until Carlton interrupted.

"I'm sorry, man. I went to physical therapy on my own for the first time. I was so proud of getting my independence that I refused to let them go with me. I scheduled it during a time when plenty of people were around. My mistake. Martin saw his chance and came by while I went to town. Tamera was in the middle of a horse therapy session. She planned on Jade's help. When she never showed up, my sister figured Jade went back to bed or was playing video games."

"Were those her typical activities since we left?" Amber's voice shook.

"No, she got up early, wanting to ride every morning. I'm sorry. Martin probably offered to ride the trail with Jade instead of allowing her to help with the therapy class. He'd ridden with us before. The girl loved the trail more than the arena. The horses he used were out in a far pasture. Tamera couldn't see them. Two mares showed up without riders an hour later. We found the government-issued SUV he arrived in parked at the end of the driveway."

"Then how did they get away?" Graham's friend wasn't providing answers soon enough.

"Either someone picked them up, or Martin had another vehicle waiting at the far edge of the farm. The SUV he left here belongs in the FBI fleet. He put an electronic requisition in for its use today. I called our boss and let him know what happened. It's time to use your team. Let the boss know your location, he'll send some agents down to help you through this mess."

"I can't believe Tamera fell for Martin's manipulation. She should have known better." Graham's fist tightened under Amber's fingers. He relaxed his grip when she gave him a reassuring touch.

"We all made mistakes." Carlton's apologetic voice crackled over the phone connection. "Headquarters assured me that Martin was the only federally related personnel involved. It looks like he worked for someone on the outside. His bank accounts received some large deposits over the last month. Let's concentrate on creating a plan of action. "

Amber could only wonder who provided the money. Probably whoever paid the minions who kept showing up like a recurring nightmare.

"The first thing that needs to be taken care of is the phony bulletin that showed up on the television at the hospital where we took Amber last night. Martin, the mole, must have hacked into some news feed in Ohio and Kentucky. I took a bullet the other day. He probably figured we'd seek medical assistance in the area."

Amber jumped when Graham barked out the orders.

"Are you all right?" Concern laced his friend's voice.

Amber wondered the same thing. Had the pain affected Graham's ability to function rationally?

"No big deal, it was just a flesh wound. Amber patched it up for me. We went to the hospital because Amber had a sprained ankle and a bad allergic reaction to poison ivy. We're both fine now."

"About that plan—" Carlton cleared his throat and paused. Amber watched her companion's stern face.

Graham looked like he was deep in thought. After a moment he spoke up. "Is Landon Clark available? He has both driving and technical skills we might need before this whole thing comes to a resolution. I worked with him a year ago. He is a straight-shooter when it comes to loyalty."

"I'll let the boss know your preference. Where should I tell Landon to meet you?" Carlton sounded relieved to have an action plan.

"We're still in Kentucky but are going to swing over into the southern tip of Virginia for our next stop. Look for an airfield somewhere in Lee County, Virginia. We'll meet him there."

Amber heard computer keys clicking in the background. "It looks like there's a small airport just south of Jonesville, Virginia. I'll ask the boss to have Agent Clark connect with you there."

"Perfect. We're headed for the home of a Winifred Grimsley, which isn't far from there. We'll talk later." Graham clicked off the phone and put the truck in motion.

Amber pursed her lips. "That name sounds vaguely familiar, but I can't place it right now."

"Maybe when we see her face to face, you'll know the woman. She worked for your father at one point." His voice sounded defeated. Amber felt at a loss herself, now that her sister was missing.

Trying to minimize her worries, Amber focused on the passing mountain scenery until she fell into a restless sleep.

~~~~~

The sense of betrayal washed over Graham like a roaring flood, threatening to drown his soul. He looked at Amber as she slept, slumped in the passenger seat. He'd started to wonder if something might grow between them. Now he wasn't so sure about taking that leap. Martin had fooled Tamera, using her loving nature, into betraying them all.

A deer darted in front of him. He slammed on the brakes. Amber moaned but kept sleeping. He didn't need to be distracted by his thoughts or by the woman sitting next to him. Instead, he concentrated on the curvy road leading over the mountains and into Virginia.

After another hour of driving, Graham pulled the truck to a stop in front of a quaint cottage. Fairytale statuary bordered the front of the home. Amber's eyes flickered open and she stretched out her arms, revealing the lingering evidence of poison ivy. She had to be in pain. Graham had chosen to let her sleep while they passed through several small towns. He'd get her some pain relief eventually.

"The time has come to figure out if you know Miss Grimsley, a former
~~~~~

employee of your father's company." Graham switched off the engine, and they exited the truck.

After following a winding path of steppingstones, through gnomes, frogs, and fairies, they knocked on the wooden-framed screen door. A musical voice answered from within. "I'll be there in a minute, magpies."

Amber burst out in laughter. "It's Miss Freddie. I'd know her voice anywhere. She was my dad's secretary when I was growing up. When Mom would come in to talk to Dad about something, Miss Freddie called me a little magpie. The woman said little children and magpies liked to chatter all the time.

Graham nodded. "I can picture you chatting away."

"We did more than just talk. She taught me how to draw and make dough sculptures during those visits. Miss Freddie kept supplies in her desk. Her influence got me started on my art journey. I missed our visits after she left the job."

Graham chuckled in spite of his resolve to not get involved with Amber. "You're chattering like a magpie right now."

She made a face at him and then turned toward the door as the sound of footsteps came closer.

A middle-aged woman pulled the door open, wearing an 'Art is SmArt' tee shirt. She smiled as she looked them over. Her gaze stopped on Amber. "Have we met before?"

Amber's grin spread across her cute face. "It's Amber Pamber, your favorite magpie."

Graham stifled his laughter behind a lifted hand.

The woman's smile faltered. She looked past their shoulders and quickly waved them inside. "I'm glad to see you, but does your father know you're here?"

"I guess you haven't heard. He passed away," Amber answered with a strained voice.

"No, we haven't been in contact for years except for —" Miss Freddie looked both relieved and guilty at the same time.

"Except for sending you some jewelry in December." Graham finished the woman's sentence and watched her closely to see how she would react.

"Yes. I —" She paused and clamped her mouth shut.

Amber held the older woman's trembling hand between her palms. "Miss Freddie, Graham is from the FBI. We know Dad did some criminal things. He left information in the jewelry that will make up for the wrongs he did."

Graham flipped open the wallet with his badge. "We need to see the jewelry and remove a clue from it that will help us figure out what Max was trying to reveal. If you know anything else that might help us, it would be to your benefit to enlighten us now, rather than later."

Her shoulders hunched. "Come and have a seat. It's a long story." She led them down an entry hallway filled with artifacts from around the world, and into a living room decorated with similar items. Masks and mosaics from several cultures filled the walls. Small statuettes sat on side tables near her couch and chairs. Graham recognized a piece from Mexican culture. His ex-fiancée had wanted to visit a Mexican resort for the honeymoon. It hadn't been a honeymoon with him in the end. He sat in a chair away from the two women, who chose to sit together on the couch. Miss Freddie looked at the ceiling and then gazed at Graham as she wrung her hands together.

"When I attended college, I majored in art education. Jobs for that type of position were few and far between. I decided to take the secretary position at MAX Enterprises. Computer art was just getting a start, and I'd taken several classes that came in handy in the world of cyber electronics. My technical skills helped me as a secretary working for Amber's father.

"Those were the good days. I enjoyed being part of the Whitney family, especially times where I could explore art with Amber. The company grew. Max hired on people like Alexander, Marcus, Victoria, and others with similar ambitions. One day, I did some work on something that felt more like hacking into someone else's account. I confronted Max about it. He threatened to fire me. I was tired of the job anyway. I counter-attacked. I always wanted to teach art instead of doing secretarial work."

"I missed you when you left." Amber put an arm around the woman's shoulders.

"I missed you, too, honey, but your father put me in a bad position, which I used to my advantage. I told him I'd keep his secret, if he'd pay for me to do my master's degree overseas, and then support me until I found a teaching position. He agreed to give me the money if I never contacted him again about what I'd seen. By then he was wealthy. He gave me plenty of funds to finish my master's and buy a few trinkets along the way." She waved to the objects and paintings around the room.

"I looked everywhere until I found my position as a traveling art teacher here in Lee County. They really needed me, and I needed them. No one else wanted to travel between three schools that were each thirty or forty miles apart. I've been happy here for over ten years.

"When I first found my teaching position, I simply sent a message to Max letting him know we were finished. I wasn't even sure Max knew where I ended up, since I didn't give him an address. Then I got the package with the teardrop pendant in it. The craftsmanship is excellent, more than the simple white stone demanded. I had no idea it hid a secret. I would have thrown it away, but there was a note threatening to expose me for my blackmailing if he ever found out I didn't hold on to the jewelry."

She looked at Graham with a sad expression. "I suppose now that you know my past, I will be facing the consequences, regardless of what he threatened."

Graham nodded. "I can't promise you anything, but if your testimony breaks up a ring of criminals, there may be some leniency." He bit back a comment about the woman using Max instead of coming to the authorities right away. She was just another example of a female that couldn't be trusted.

He studied the woman in front of him as he continued the conversation. "Amber made the jewelry at her father's request. She didn't realize until recently he'd added something inside of it to prevent further criminal activity from among his cohorts."

"Well done, Magpie." She sighed. "Now, what is going to happen to me?"

Graham crossed his arms. "You were wise to get out while you could, but it would have prevented a lot of problems if you contacted law enforcement at the time the crime happened. As I mentioned before, if you will testify in court about what you saw at MAX Enterprises, the information will help your case."

"I hope so. I love teaching my little magpies here in Lee County."

"I'm sure they are blessed to have you. You need to contact a substitute teacher for the last few weeks of school. I'll call my boss and see if we can put you in protective custody until we can solve this case." Graham pulled out the satellite phone and started putting in the number.

"Since Max is no longer around, won't I be safe? I need to be here for my students. They're all the family I have." The woman looked about ready to cry.

"We hope you'll be back to them before next school year. Right now, there are other dangerous people out there who already shot at the two of us. Since you can testify to Max's wrongdoing, you need to rely on the FBI to protect you." Graham shook his head at her lack of understanding of the situation.

Miss Freddie's face paled. Graham walked into the entry hall as his call went through.

"Hey, Boss. I'm checking to make sure you put out a missing child bulletin on Jade." His superior responded in the affirmative. "Good, because we've got another problem."

Chapter Fifteen

Amber stood and pretended to admire Miss Freddie's art collection while she edged closer to the hallway. As she eavesdropped on Graham's side of the phone conversation, she felt the chasm widen between the agent and herself. He was job centered. Her role in the case provided the only reason they traveled together. That should be reassuring but somehow the knowledge wasn't comforting. Jade's kidnapping was more than a business transaction. She tried not to think about it, but the thoughts in her brain kept swirling back to her crime-solving partner.

"Do you like him?" Miss Freddie interrupted the storm that waged war with Amber's good sense.

"He's a nice guy, but liking him in the way you're probably thinking isn't possible. He only thinks of me as part of this assignment. Once this is over, my name will just be something for him to write down in a case-closed file. Besides, after seeing the way my father treated Mom and me, trusting a man with my heart is difficult." She wandered around the room, admiring more of the art. "Did you ever have a desire to marry?"

"Wow. That was a big jump from talk about liking someone to marriage." Miss Freddie ran her fingers across a woven tapestry. She paused to look at Amber. "I always felt like I was hiding from your father or someone worse. I didn't want to attach myself to any man and have to drag him into a world of being cautious or hidden away."

She crossed her arms. "I dated a policeman when all this was going down. Max hinted that if I leaked anything to my boyfriend, bad things would happen to him. I cared about the guy. I dropped him for his own good. I understood then that I needed to get away from the whole situation. When Max agreed to pay for my master's degree, I ran as far away as I could and hoped my troubles were over."

"I'm sorry my father ruined your life. Maybe it will change when this case is resolved." Amber tried to not dwell on her father's influence on her own life.

"Maybe, but as you heard, I made choices that helped put me where I am. However, I've done well all by myself. I have my art and my students. My only regret is not going to the authorities. Now I have no choice. It feels like a load has fallen off my shoulders since I've owned up to the past. How about your life once this is all over?"

"Thanks to your influence, I pursued a career in art. I specialized in lapidary. I've been teaching at the college level. I have plans to go into business for myself soon. My studio store is ready for a grand opening once this mess is cleared up." Amber hoped her shop was still intact since she deserted it after the first attack.

"Wonderful. I am happy you found your place in the world." Miss Freddie leaned closer and hugged her.

"I am too. The sooner we get all this behind us, the better. May I take a look inside the pendant Dad sent you?"

"Sure." Miss Freddie led Amber toward the back of the cottage and into a room decorated as a study. Awards for being an outstanding teacher lined one of the walls. There were also plaques honoring entries in art shows and competitions. Amber noticed a shelf with multiple copies of children's books authored by various writers. Someone named Winnie Gee had illustrated all the volumes in the collection. Something clicked in Amber's mind. Miss Freddie had drawn entertaining creatures for her during Mom's visits with Dad. Had she channeled those doodles into illustrating?

"Have you been moonlighting, Miss Winifred Grimsley? Or should I say, Winnie Gee?" Amber pulled one of the books from the shelf and held it in front of Miss Freddie's face.

"You know what they say about teacher salaries—" The woman shrugged and opened a drawer in her desk.

"Yeah, I know. That's one of the reasons I started my studio. College instructor salaries are worse than public school pay." Amber grinned and pointed. Miss Freddie's computer had sprung to life when she bumped it on the way up from retrieving the piece of jewelry from the drawer. The monitor and a tablet near the computer revealed an illustration of a crafty-looking fox. The digital art reflected the same style as the illustrations in the book she held. "You are so busted, my friend."

"I confess." Miss Freddy held her hands in the air with the pendant hanging from her fingers.

"Hold it right there and tell me what you need to confess." Graham entered the room with his gun at his side, looking ready to take on a criminal. Both women looked at each other and laughed until tears rolled down their cheeks.

"This is not the time to be funny, ladies. If she has something to confess, I need to know what is going on."

"Miss Winifred G. has some explaining to do, but only to a bunch of misled children who want to know who the real illustrator of this book is." Amber turned the book toward him.

Graham's eyebrows raised. "Are you Winnie Gee? The boss's grandkids love your illustrations. The last time I was at his house, the boys asked me to read that exact book. He bought the story for one of their birthdays. My boss is going to be happy to meet you."

"I didn't know I'd be meeting anyone's boss." Miss Freddie ran her hands over her messy bun.

"Once I mentioned your name, he said he'd be helping out on the case. Most of our team is searching for Jade, Amber's kidnapped half-sister. The boss is flying in with agent Landon Clark later today. Landon will travel with Amber and me. Our boss will stay with you while he arranges a safe place for you to stay until your testimony is needed."

"Is it possible I can finish up my school year? There are several projects my students need to wrap up before school is out at the end of the month." A frown creased Miss Freddie's forehead.

"You can work that out with the boss, and maybe his grandkids. Do yourself a favor and don't mention his wife. She passed away last year from cancer. He doesn't like talking about her or the disease. Asking about the grandkids is a safe subject."

"If he looks as good as Agent Graham here, you may have to rethink your single status, Miss Freddie." Amber wanted to clamp her hand over her mouth. She couldn't believe the words spewing from her lips.

"Umm, is that the jewelry Max sent you?"

The two ladies raised their eyebrows at Graham's attempt to change the subject. Miss Freddie handed the piece to Amber. Both onlookers leaned over the younger woman's shoulder as she carefully released the stone from its setting and opened the latch for the hidden compartment.

Miss Freddie gasped when Amber pulled out the diode and held it in the air. "I haven't seen one of those in years."

"Can you give us a hint about this piece?" Amber handed the diode to Miss Freddie.

"Max kept them lying around as conversation pieces. This little gadget is actually an important part of electronic history. They aren't used much anymore, but quartz crystal transistors and diodes were a big part of the golden years of radio and early television. Max picked up a bunch of them at a flea market and put them in glass jars around the reception room so people would wonder what they were. Do you remember playing with them, Amber?"

"I remember making a mosaic with some of them during one of our craft sessions."

Miss Freddie borrowed the eyepiece and looked closer at the diode. "This looks slightly different from the old ones we had in the office. My guess would be Max had it specially made to fit a specific device, but I have no idea what that would be. It wouldn't surprise me if he made this himself. He was very talented, just like his daughter."

"I wish Dad had been trustworthy." That would have made Amber's life easier on so many fronts. "I may have gotten a steady hand from my father, but I don't want to claim any other of his so-called abilities."

Miss Freddie handed the diode and magnifier back to Amber and picked up the loose stone and empty silver setting. "Please tell me you can put this back together. Now that I know you made the jewelry, I'll treasure it as a gift from my favorite magpie."

"I'll fix it right up, just for you, my very first art teacher." Amber laid out her tools and carefully reset the stone. She sensed Graham's presence as he watched her work. Then he wandered into the other room with his phone to his ear.

Voices from a news channel sounded from Miss Freddie's front room. The two women chatted about art and education for several hours. They laughed over student stories. Amber admired her mentor's artwork and digital tools until a loud knock at the front door echoed through the home. The same fear she saw reflected on Miss Freddie's face sent a chill through Amber's body. They both stood, ready for fight or flight.

~~~~~

Graham looked through the peephole in Miss Freddie's solid door, his hand resting on his shoulder holster. He'd insisted on closing the wooden door earlier, unlike the open screen door they'd first entered. Two familiar faces appeared. Tension rolled off his back. He'd been carrying this case alone for too long. The sudden silence in the other room told him the women had their own load of worries.

"It's all right, ladies, backup has arrived." He swung the door open and clapped the reinforcements from his FBI team on their backs. "I'm so glad to see you two."

Landon looked pleased to see him and thumped Graham's back in return. "Likewise."

Graham's boss, Kent Russell, scanned the room with a frown. "Where is the witness?"

"Come on back to her office and I'll introduce everyone." Graham led the two men down the hallway.

As they entered the room, Miss Freddie stiffened. The scowl coming from his normally calm leader left Graham filled with curiosity. No wonder the woman looked unhappy. "Ladies, this is my boss, Kent Russell, and my fellow agent, Landon Clark." He laid a hand on Amber's shoulder. "This is Amber Whitney who has helped me find the clues that Max, her father, left behind. Our witness needing protection is Winifred Grimsley."

"Miss Whitney." Kent nodded. "Miss Grimsley. It's been a while." Kent Russell's voice clanged out like coated steel.

Miss Freddie stammered something that sounded like "Kent."

Graham had only experienced that tone of voice from his boss when he messed up an operation. Did Kent know the woman from somewhere
~~~~~

else? His comment about it being a while seemed odd. Something was off, but he knew better than to question the boss when the man exhibited a dark mood. Since his wife had passed, the gloomy temperament manifested itself more often than before.

Amber nodded in response to the introduction and turned a troubled gaze in Graham's direction. He shrugged since he had no idea what his boss was thinking. Miss Freddie just stared at Kent Russell, her face turning shades of red before she paled and looked down at her wringing hands.

"I don't need to hear your excuses, not now, not ever." Kent leaned closer to the woman and said something Graham couldn't make out. He turned his back on Miss Freddie. "Give us an update on the situation, Graham. Then you three can be on your way. I'll deal with our witness later."

"Sure. Let's meet around the kitchen table so we can share the details." Graham led the three of them from the office. Miss Freddie scurried past him, cleared her table, and shoved a canister of cookies onto the table with trembling hands.

Amber edged closer to Graham before they took their seats. "What's going on with your boss?"

"I have no idea, but we better let that snarling puppy alone for now. Have you got the diodes handy?"

"Sure do, even the one we just got." She slid into a chair beside his and snagged a cookie. A derisive snort from Kent, followed by Miss Freddie's huffy departure covered Amber's mumbled thanks to the baker.

"So what do you have so far? Fill us in so we can plan a strategy for getting this case over and done." Kent's no-nonsense voice had returned without the harshness heard in the other room.

"When I worked as Max's bodyguard, he mentioned the possibility of wanting to share the names of his fellow cyber criminals but seemed cautious about just handing them over. We've learned he has a past of playing games with information. Max asked Amber to make jewelry with compartments. Later, he had Amber's Uncle Warren add a deeper place in the jewelry for hiding diodes. We think the diodes will help reveal the names of those involved in a cybercrime ring."

Amber opened the pouch and spread the tiny pieces out for Kent to study. Graham continued. "They may have something to do with an electronic device, but we have no idea yet. Martin Johnson, acting as a mole, electronically traced our movements until recently. He revealed himself by kidnapping Amber's half-sister, Jade. He also managed to put out a BOLO on the two of us."

Landon entered the conversation. "We were able to trace Martin's activities and put up firewalls preventing him from accessing our network. I personally made sure that his false bulletin is not out there anymore. Jesslyn and Brittany are headed for Carlton's to start working the kidnapping case." Landon picked up one of the diodes and examined it. "This looks like old tech, but there's something different about it I can't place."

"That's what Miss Freddie said." Amber's comment caused the frown to return to Kent's face.

"Let's stick to official information. What's your plan from here, Graham?" Kent crossed his arms and glared at Amber, who stared right back at the man.

Graham swallowed the urge to chuckle at the brave woman giving his boss the teacher look. Instead, he cleared his throat and described his plan. "While the other agents look for our kidnap victim, the three of us will search for the rest of the jewelry. Our last stop will be at Gorge Bluff, Alabama. Hopefully someone along our travels will have more information about how the diodes fit together, perhaps on a motherboard or some such device. Max hinted that the names of his fellow cyber criminals would be revealed by the end of our journey. I can only pray we figure this out before someone else does."

The boss turned away from Amber. "Keep me informed. I'll stay with the witness until we move her to a safe house. The local division met us at the airport with an SUV. You three take that vehicle. I'll use what you drove."

"The truck belongs to my mother's friend, Harold. I trust you'll get it back to him in good shape." Amber's raised eyebrows forced a nod from his boss. Graham looked up at the wall above the table and concentrated on one of the art pieces to control the laughter bubbling in his belly. Not everyone could control his boss. Amber managed to do it with a look.

Landon stood beside the table. "I'm ready when you two are."

Graham joined him. "We just have to transfer our bags from the truck and we'll be ready."

Amber laid her set of truck keys on the table and headed down the hallway. "I'm saying goodbye to my friend first. I'll be out in a minute."

Graham hit the unlock button for the truck's remote and added his key to the ones she left. Kent handed him two fobs for the SUV.

"Take care, boss. Hopefully this case will be over soon."

"Time will tell. Sometimes it takes years before the whole truth is revealed." Kent slumped back in his chair, looking worn out, the steel in his voice gone.

"We'll keep you informed." Graham took one more look at Kent and wondered what was really going on. Amber stepped back into the room with a couple of children's books and a tube of cortisone cream. When she nodded goodbye toward his boss, her look was one of pity. What had made her attitude change so quickly?

"Do you want to tell me what's going on?" Graham asked.

"Later. Let's just say that Miss Freddie and Kent have a lot of catching up to do. They knew each other at one point. Your boss will let you know the details when the time is right." Great, the mysteries were piling up. He followed her outside. They transferred what they had into the SUV.

Landon manned the wheel as they pulled away from the house. "Where to, boss man?"

"I'm not the boss. I don't want to be after the display back there." They both laughed.

"Yeah, he groused the whole flight down. He kept trying to find information on the internet about Winifred Grimsley. Nothing popped up other than a reference to being an art teacher in this corner of Virginia. Now, where are we headed to next?"

"Take the main road out of Jonesville and turn west toward Middlesboro. We'll head south from there until I give you other directions."

"It looked like the boss was pretty rattled by the woman back at the house. Did she say anything about knowing who he was?" Landon waited for a couple of fast-moving trucks to pass and then pulled out onto the road.

"I'm pretty sure I just referred to Kent as the boss until they met. She looked pretty surprised when she saw him walk in the door." Graham rubbed his arm and felt relieved that it seemed to be healing.

Landon did a quick glance in the back seat. "Hey, Amber, did she say anything to you about knowing him?"

"Not that I'm sharing. Trust me when I tell you their past won't provide a solution for your case. My lips are sealed until those two let you know more." Amber zipped her lips and grinned.

Graham wanted to react to her smug remark but decided not to pursue whatever she knew for now. He leaned back against the seat, glad to let someone else drive. Relaxation didn't come. His thoughts drifted to other things, like how they could use the 'sort of antique' diodes to solve Max's riddle.

As they passed over a high mountain, he looked down into the peaceful valley below. His mind once again wandered to Kent Russell and Winifred Grimsley. He wondered if those two were having a peaceful discussion. From what he'd observed, Graham doubted their words were happy ones.

Chapter Sixteen

Amber's ears popped as the SUV headed down the curvy mountain road toward lower elevations. They'd cut off the main road a while back. Besides the ear discomfort, waves of heat and uneasiness boiled in her stomach and started up her throat. Rolling down the window and pushing her nose out for fresh air helped some. She should have known better than to be in the back seat of a vehicle on a mountain road. It produced the same nausea as a roller coaster.

"Are you okay back there?" Graham swiveled in his seat.

"No, can we stop before—" She held her hand over her mouth as she started heaving.

Landon braked quickly. She stepped out of the car and leaned over until her stomach settled. Both men stood back, looking helpless.

"Thanks, guys." She hoped her sarcasm came through loud and clear. "It's just a little motion sickness. You don't have to worry about catching a plague."

"I should have remembered. Can we do anything to help?" Graham swiped a hand across his mouth and looked a little pale as he observed her pitiful condition.

"Yeah, I'm calling shotgun from here on out unless I'm in the driver's seat. It wouldn't hurt to turn up the air conditioner fan speed either and take the curves a little slower."

"I'll do anything you need." Graham offered his hand as he escorted her to the front passenger seat.

"Ah, so that's how it is. I should probably take a turn in the rear so you two can have time to chat." A wide grin spread across Landon's face before he ducked into the backseat.

Amber felt a different kind of heat flow through her body.

Graham grabbed Landon's door and sputtered out an answer before she could think of a rebuttal. "No, Landon, it is not what you think. She is in our custody. We need to take care of her. That is all."

She should have agreed with the statement, but a sliver of irritation skittered up her backbone and out of her mouth. "Yup, take good care of me or I'll report you to the boss for the appropriate discipline."

Graham lifted both hands in the air and stepped back. "Yes, ma'am, only appropriate behavior from here on out." He stomped around the SUV to plop into the driver's seat.

Silent tension filled the atmosphere inside the SUV for the next hour. High winds blew from air vents as they slowly descended the rest of the mountain and entered an area of rolling hills. Amber kept her gaze glued to the front window, anticipating each turn. Deep breaths of cool air helped keep the nausea at bay until the road settled into something bearable.

If only she could handle her emotions by blowing on them for a cool down. She needed to accept that it would be impossible for the two of them to have a relationship. He'd pretty well stated he wasn't interested. Why did she even care? It didn't help that he was a handsome, kind, and caring person. She needed to treat him like poison ivy and stand back. Otherwise, she'd be miserable and heartsick. That way he could do his job, solve Dad's mess, and rescue Jade from the kidnapper.

A welcome sign announced they were entering a small town. Landon broke the icy silence. "I could use something to eat, if this town is big enough for some fast food."

Graham gave Amber a brief look. "Can your stomach handle food now?"

"Some protein and starch would be nice. We've only eaten snacks the last day or two." The tension that held her stiff flowed out of her body. They could still have a normal conversation about basic needs.

A few blocks later, Graham pulled into a restaurant. It wasn't a name brand, but it claimed to have the best burgers in town. The scent of grilled meat emanated from the building. The parking lot was full, a clear sign of good food. Amber heard her stomach growl and hoped it hadn't been loud enough for the others to hear. Based on Graham's chuckle, she knew her wishes were in vain.

"Let's go inside to eat. I'm tired of sitting in something with four wheels." She also needed a little time away from her driver for the last few days, but didn't dare mention her thoughts aloud.

Landon stood in line to place their order while Graham chose a table. She headed for the restroom and hid out until someone knocked on the door. Amber splashed water on her face and walked to the table where the guys had placed Styrofoam containers of burgers and fries.

She chose the empty seat next to Landon and sipped from her strawberry shake. Both men bowed their heads briefly before digging into their burgers. She thanked the Lord for the food while praying for Jade, continued safety, and a quick resolution to the case. She looked up and inhaled the smell of ketchup and pickles as she opened her mouth wide to savor the taste. The burger satisfied the longing for something substantial in her empty stomach.

She sighed and felt a little awkward, noticing several people watching her with interest. Graham's body tensed. She glanced at her shirt, wondering if ketchup dribbled down her front. When she looked up, several families wrapped up their meals and hurried from the restaurant.

Landon stopped mid-sentence in their conversation about some kind of training. He looked at the exiting diners. A couple of wide-eyed teens aimed phones her way and snapped pictures, then left their table in a mess. Two clerks behind the counter alternated between peering into a phone and looking at the table where she sat.

"Let's get out of here." Graham's voice was stern. He placed himself between Amber and the remaining diners. She grabbed her container of food and stood behind him.

Amber found herself wedged between the two agents as they walked from the restaurant. The remaining restaurant patrons moved out of their way like a tidal wave. Some had their phones to their ears, whispering information to someone.

As they hustled from the restaurant, Amber heard one man say, "I just spotted those people that were on the internet. They're here at Best Burgers. About that reward—"

Amber jumped into the SUV and put her box of food on her lap. She peeked out her window while fastening her seatbelt. Teenaged paparazzi stood behind cars and in the restaurant's windows, talking, snapping, and searching on their phones. Had the world gone mad? "I know you don't want my phone on right now, but it might be a good idea if I checked my social media."

"Help yourself, but keep it short." Graham pulled out from the restaurant and onto the road.

While she waited for her phone to wake up, Amber looked at her side mirror and noticed an older model truck fall in behind them. Great, now even average citizens were out to get them for some so-called reward.

Bells rang as her phone woke up with messages pending and texts from her artists, wondering when they were going to hear more about the grand opening. Disregarding those, she opened one of her social media accounts and stared at her image.

"Hey, Graham, I thought the FBI was going to take care of that phony BOLO on the two of us." She angled her phone so both men could get a glimpse of the images she'd seen in the hospital.

Landon groaned. "I took care of stopping it myself. Even though we ceased the BOLO, it's hard to put a stopper on the fake messages blasting across social media these days. I'll call someone in the main office and get them to contact the major media outlets. Maybe they can stop the madness."

"In the meantime, whoever is following us knows exactly where we were for the last half hour." Amber flipped through several photos of them eating burgers and held her phone so they could see.

"This mission just got blasted out of the water. With our faces showing up everywhere, I won't be able to do another undercover assignment for a long time." Graham smacked the steering wheel. "We'll be lucky to get this one completed without a lot of interference from the public."

Amber bent over her phone and watched as more pictures popped up on her screen. "It looks like our followers in the truck are making sure everyone knows they're on our tail. They took a picture of the tags on this vehicle and said they're claiming the reward."

"Hit the comment button and tell them to back off, or they'll be in big trouble with the FBI." Graham pushed the SUV to a higher speed as they headed out of town.

Amber tapped the reply into her phone. The answer came back in the form of the truck's bumper hitting their SUV. Amber's phone flew out of her hands and hit the floor. She leaned over to get it as a bullet ripped through the back window and out of the windshield in front of her seat.

~~~~~

Graham pressed the pedal down to the floor. "Are you two all right?"

"Affirmative." Landon's one word answer sounded muffled, but the click of a gun told him the agent prepared to take a stand against their attackers, probably from the cover of the space between the two seats.

His heartbeat tanked as he waited for Amber to answer. Finally she groaned. "How badly are you hurt?"

She sat up in her seat. Her pale face was covered in red streaks. *No.*

"Keep your head down. We don't want you to take another shot."

She leaned back down but started giggling. Her body shook. Shock must have settled in. Her laughter grew louder.

"Take a breath, honey. This isn't the time to go into your stressed-out humor."

Another shot thumped against the SUV's side. Landon's image popped up briefly in his rearview mirror as his fellow agent fired a warning shot. His concern for Amber warred with the stress of keeping their SUV on the road as it took a second tap on the bumper. She quit laughing and wiped the red from her bent-over face with a napkin. At least she wasn't going to faint from the sight of her own blood.

"Speed up." Landon's voice broke into Graham's thoughts. "Let me know when you can see the whole front of their truck. I'll try to get a shot into either a tire or radiator."

Graham complied. After they rounded a curve, he pulled ahead of the truck on a straight stretch. Landon took his shot. The truck slowed to a stop. Amber retched on the floor.

"I'm so sorry." Her voice sounded weak. "This car is going to stink."

"Save your strength, sweetheart. We're going to get you to a hospital."
~~~~~

Graham clasped her shoulder and gave it a reassuring squeeze. He didn't want to lose this woman. He'd been fighting the attraction for the whole trip. The sight of her blood gave him a whole new perspective.

"Hospitals don't usually treat people for motion sickness." She sat up in her seat and looked at him like he'd gone crazy. She swiped at a remaining drop of red on her cheek and wiped it on a napkin. "What are you looking at?"

"You're bleeding. We need to get you some medical help."

"This mess on my face is ketchup from my lunch. The storm in my belly died on the last curve. No need for another hospital visit, especially with a fake BOLO to freak people out."

Tension fell from his shoulders.

She added, "I was worried about you, too, Graham."

The bullet hadn't hit her. He reached for her hand, resting on the console between them, and she accepted the gesture. A warm feeling swept up his arm. Graham sat taller in the seat.

Landon cleared his throat from the back seat. "What's our next step, love birds?"

Amber's palm relaxed. She began inching away. Graham held tight, squeezing her hand before glancing her way and releasing their clasped fingers. He noticed a surprised smile as she turned to watch the road.

Graham pulled his empty hand off the console and set it on the steering wheel. Focusing on driving and answering Landon, he snapped out an order. "Contact headquarters. Tell them to take care of that social media blitz. I want to see a retraction on every site and station by the time the evening news hits. Until then, we need to lay low, maybe take a hike in a lesser-known forest. I'll expect a new vehicle before this day is over."

"Yes sir." Landon punched numbers into his phone and had most of the details ironed out in less than half an hour. His phone rang shortly afterward. Landon shared the instructions to pull into a nearby state park and wait for a local law enforcement officer to connect them with a new vehicle.

Graham parked the SUV and walked around it, surveying the damage. Broken glass in both the front and back windows, a bullet hole on one side, and scrapes on the bumper gave testimony to their near escape. He'd make sure the local law enforcement knew about their side of the story when those would-be vigilantes had their say.

A trailhead near where they parked beckoned to him. He needed time to think. Amber had stepped into the park's restroom to clean up. Landon indicated it would be at least another hour before their new ride would arrive.

"I'm going to take that hike. I won't go far." He crammed the cowboy hat down on his head and trudged down the trail. He'd make sure he repaid Amber's friend, Loretta, for the hat or purchased something similar when the case closed. For now, the head-covering hid his face from any other vigilantes who hadn't gotten the message about the false BOLO. Maybe the hat would help keep his head on straight.

The sign at the start of the path indicated it led to a waterfall about a quarter mile away. The winding descent required his concentration. It felt good not to think about anything regarding the case for a few minutes. Green leaves rustled in the warm breeze.

His thoughts wavered between nature and the woman who had taken over his life in such a short time. In the few days since they'd met, she'd proven herself an intelligent and capable person. So far she'd been truthful and open about everything except whatever she knew about the boss and Miss Freddie. He liked being in the loop, but maybe that truly was none of his business. He didn't share much about his past either.

The waterfall came into view. It wasn't huge, but the sound called to him. A bench sat at the edge of the stream below the falls. He took a seat and attempted to clear his mind by listening to the swooshing water. He closed his eyes and sat until he heard someone else on the trail behind him. Tension roared louder than the sound of the soothing falls. He turned, prepared to face possible danger.

"Relax, cowboy, it's just me." Amber approached, wearing the floppy hat she'd picked up at the yard sale. At least that was where he thought she'd gotten it. He'd been in major pain during that event. She slid onto the far end of the bench. Her fingers twisted the cloth at the hem of her shirt. The wide brim covered her face so he couldn't see her expression.

For a few moments they sat in silence. The waterfall no longer seemed like a source of peace. A deeper yearning filled his heart. Amber was safe. She sat beside him. Whether he wanted to admit it or not, his heart beat with affection when she sat nearby. He crossed his arms and tried to focus on the water flowing downstream.

She pulled off her hat and looked his way. Wisps of hair blew in the breeze. He shoved his hands into his armpits and clamped down the urge to tuck the hair behind her ears. Amber cleared her throat. He took a deep breath.

"Back there in the car, you called me honey and sweetheart. Was that just your southern charm coming through, or did you mean anything more?" She looked vulnerable. She deserved the truth, even though she'd given him an out. He dropped his hands to his lap and extended one to her. When she scooted closer and placed her palm across his, it felt like a wall had fallen.

"I'm fighting with myself on that one. The truth is, I am attracted to you, but events in my past make me cautious about being in a relationship."

"I can relate to that. My Dad set a poor example for me about the trustworthiness of men."

"I'm sorry. Several years ago, I gave romance a try. The wedding planning was in progress when she let me know I had a choice between my job and our future. Her father created a well-paid position in his business so she could continue living at her accustomed economic level. The woman wanted me at her side during social events. She didn't like when I had to leave town for a case."

"Your fiancée must have loved you very much. She wanted you near her." Amber looked down at their joined hands.

"I thought so, but when I told her I didn't want to take the position with her father's business, the woman dropped me like a hot piece of coal. It wasn't long before she turned her interests to my brother. They were married on the date we had planned for our own marriage." Graham watched the water rippling by. He felt cleansed from the past by admitting to what had happened.

"Ouch, that had to hurt. Family holidays must be awkward." Amber grimaced.

"Not anymore. She dumped my brother for someone further up the corporate ladder. He lost his job with her father's company. My sibling was glad to find out his former position was open at the time. He apologized for getting involved with her. I told him I was sorry for introducing her into our family. She hurt us both. Up to this point, we've both been confirmed bachelors."

"Up to this point?" Pink blossomed across her cheeks. Graham gave in and tugged a flying curl behind her ear. His hand lingered on her cheek until she looked down.

He turned away and focused on the waterfall. Her hand still warmed his. "Yeah, since I met you, I've been fighting with myself about whether I'm ready for a relationship. I'm leaning toward the possibility of getting to know you better when this whole ordeal is over."

Her hand tightened in his. "I'd be open to that opportunity too. You've proven you are a man who is trustworthy."

Graham released her hand and wrapped his arm around her shoulders as he pulled her close to his side. He pushed back the cowboy hat and leaned his forehead against hers.

His phone rang. Sirens echoed through the trees. Graham answered the call and heard Landon's voice.

"It looks like the local cops have arrived. Hopefully they got the message about the BOLO removal, but if they didn't, you two stay hidden. The regional division should be here soon with your next car. You can go on if I get detained." Landon's connection dropped along with Graham's gut.

Amber met his concerned expression. He'd held the phone close to both their ears and figured she'd overheard the conversation. *Please Lord, keep Landon from harm.*

Chapter Seventeen

"Did you hear?"

Amber nodded, missing his closeness as he continued.

"We need to take our time getting back to the parking lot. Landon will cover for us if it becomes necessary. I'd like to be close enough to help if he needs us, though. In the meantime, I'm going to call headquarters and make sure they contacted the local law enforcement again or if they've heard anything more about Jade, Martin, or the people who started this whole thing." He stepped away and spoke into the phone.

Amber walked back toward the stream near the waterfall. She watched a small eddy spinning near the edge of the water. Her heart was doing some spinning of its own. For the first time in her life, since being a sixteen-year-old, she'd opened herself up to a possible relationship. Her happiness swirled with doubts about making the wrong decision. As she watched Graham talking on the phone, she prayed she'd made the right choice, because she had never met a man quite like him. He'd broken through her barrier of mistrust.

Graham darkened his phone, only to revive it again as more ringing pierced the air. Moments later, a handsome smile crossed his face as he walked closer and held out his hand to Amber. "That's great, Landon. We'll be there once we climb the trail."

As they stepped up the path, Amber felt lighter than she had in a long time. The incline seemed easier to climb than she thought it would. Leaning on Graham relieved the fading pain in her ankle. The blue sky glistened with billowing white clouds. A canopy of green leaves spread their shade across the ground. Birds filled the air with chatter. Graham's hand warmed hers the whole way to the parking lot.

When they reached the trailhead, Landon's face looked like a thundercloud about to burst. He held her phone in his hand. Amber's messy cell and attached wallet must have been hard to clean up. Then she remembered she'd been looking at social media and had forgotten to turn the device off.

"You got some messages right after I called. I heard the phone ping and picked it up out of the debris. The texts sound threatening. There's a picture of an upset young girl. The photo looks like the pictures the agency shared of your half-sister Jade. The images show her tied to a chair with a gag around her mouth. Someone wants you to tell what you know, or they will hurt Jade."

Amber sighed. How long could this go on and how many people would face harm before they found the rest of Max's clues? They'd left one Mrs. Whitney in the hospital with a promise from Officer Hollingsworth for the woman's safety. Graham had been injured and Jade kidnapped. She wasn't doing too well herself, between poison ivy, a twisted ankle, and growing worries.

"I feel so frustrated by this. Maybe the time to just give up has come. I don't want anyone else in danger."

"If we don't get the information Max left for us, even more people will suffer. Jade is a tough young lady. We have several of our team in the field looking for her now." Graham laid a hand on her shoulder. She leaned into him, her arms crossed.

Landon continued sharing information. "Right now, our focus has to be on keeping Amber safe. Those who are looking for her have seen the posts on social media. They know approximately where we are. Based on their last text, they seem capable of recognizing when your phone is active. The local cop over there got a message from his office about more misleading information while he was talking to me. Good thing he'd already confirmed our status as agents with the FBI. Now, these criminals have blitzed social media with information about the abduction of Amber and Jade by her father's rogue bodyguard. They're offering a reward for her return."

"Whoever they are, they should be the ones facing kidnapping charges because of Jade." Amber's blood boiled. She'd only known her half-sister for a short time. She didn't want to lose the girl.

"Kidnapping will be one of many charges brought against them before this is all over." Graham reached for her hand. She accepted his gesture. Amber needed the strength his support provided. Graham focused on Landon. "Any news from headquarters or the boss?"

"Nothing from the boss, which is strange. I talked to one of our trusted techies and we're turning off Amber's phone. Tech will make it look like the device is on. They'll fix it with a VPN so the phone location shows us headed in the opposite direction. All messages will go to headquarters instead of her cell."

"What about my personal messages? I'm trying to start a business, if this whole affair doesn't blow my studio out of the water." Thoughts of losing all she'd worked for made worry stomp a frenzied dance across a growing headache.

"You should be able to retrieve all of those once this is over, if you don't end up in some kind of protective custody until a court date can be set." Landon's statement caught her off guard.

Would her fledgling business sink like the *Titanic* because she wouldn't be around to man the ship? Amber's shoulders tightened until Graham wrapped an arm around them.

Landon didn't seem to notice Amber's reactions. "For now, we need to get you two into some different outfits. Officer Anderson over there will take you to her home and help you get a new look. The local division is bringing two vehicles and a female agent. I'm going to drive away with her in a different direction from you two. We'll take Amber's deactivated phone with us on the remote possibility that the cybercriminals have been able to track it with everything off. The agency will bring the other vehicle to the officer's home. We're hoping this will divert our criminals onto a different path."

Amber held out her hand. "Let me have my phone so I can get my ID and money from the wallet." Landon hesitantly turned it over. It still reeked of ketchup and the contents of her stomach. She had to fight the desire to get sick again. "There are several memos on my cell that are important to starting my new business. Please don't let anyone destroy them."

Landon nodded. "I will do my best." He watched her remove the requested items from the wallet, but then stopped her when she pulled out a credit card. "I'll keep your card. We might buy something small with it to throw our criminals further off track." He lifted Graham's cowboy hat from his head and stuffed it down on his own. He didn't look half the cowboy that Graham had. "I'll take this hat since it's gone viral on the internet. Yours too." Landon held out his hand toward Amber.

She handed the wide-brimmed hat over and stuffed the contents of her wallet into her jeans pocket, next to the pouch of diodes. The aura of being exposed to the world made her shudder. She looked around at their surroundings, before focusing on Landon. "We borrowed the cowboy hat. Make sure it gets back to me when this is all over so I can get it back to my friend."

Wondering if she would make it through the ordeal, she shared her friend's address with the agent. He assured her he'd take care of both head coverings. She walked to the SUV and pulled out the oversize bag with Mom's and her friend's clothing. She decided to keep the bag for a purse since she no longer would have access to her cell phone's wallet. The borrowed clothing easily fit into one of the plastic store bags they'd collected. She handed the clothing to Landon with the same instructions for Graham's hat and a note saying she still had the purse.

Graham paced nearby. He ran his fingers through his cropped hair. His full beard had grown during the last few days, revealing reddish tints matching his honey-toned hair. A scowl crossed his face. He was not a cowboy anymore. Maybe she should call him Red-beard the pirate. Though, he'd need an eye patch for his disguise. Then he could be her buccaneer. She started to laugh but contained it to a chuckle. No way was she sharing her current ramblings aloud.

~~~~~

Graham stopped pacing. If he kept it up, he'd end up digging a hole that reached down to groundwater. Amber finished talking to Landon and looked lost as she scanned the forest and the road that ran next to the park. He needed to get her out of sight of any passing cars. Landon was already in their battered vehicle with the cowboy hat on his head. He'd be a sitting duck if someone caught up to him before the replacement vehicle arrived. Even though several police cars sat nearby, the members of his team were all out in the open.

Help us get through this, Lord.

Amber looked ready to go into one of her nervous comedy routines when an unmarked squad car stopped next to her. Graham grabbed her hand after they ducked into the back seat and sank down low.

"Make yourselves comfortable back there, folks. I'm Lieutenant Michelle Anderson. My husband and I aren't too different in size from the two of you. We'll get you all set for your next step."

"Thank you, officer, we appreciate your help." Graham understood all too well that the woman was going beyond her required duty.

"I'm glad to help out. We don't usually get much FBI action in our little burg. Sorry about our local vigilantes. Those two will be doing some jail time until we can figure out what charges they receive. They were a couple of out of work guys looking to make some fast cash with the reward money." She put the squad car in motion.

"That's too bad. They never would have seen any reward." Graham surveyed the parking lot one more time, hoping Landon would be safe.

"Yeah, if they hadn't resorted to using their guns, we wouldn't charge them with anything major." The officer put the squad car in motion. Amber groaned as they turned out of the parking lot.

Graham remembered her motion sickness. They didn't need a repeat performance. "Here, Amber, position your head so you can get some of the airflow coming from the console between the seats. That way you can see where we're going. Lieutenant Anderson, would you mind upping the air conditioner?"

"Sure, you wouldn't be the first passengers to have a problem with my backseat, though most were inebriated at the time." She reached for the controls and blasted them with a chilly breeze. Amber relaxed into his side. He leaned his head near hers. She didn't back away. Cozy warmth flowed through his body despite the freezing air blowing through her hair and into his face. Amber started giggling.

"What is your warped sense of humor thinking about now?"

"I'm queen of the world. Or perhaps you should be saying I'm king
~~~~~

of the world." She stretched her arms wide across the back of both front seats and stuck her nose near the vent located in the console.

"I hope we have better luck than Jack and Rose did on the *Titanic*." Graham hated to bring her back down, but her analogy wasn't giving him any comfort.

"Hey, I'm living in the moment and enjoying the sea breeze in my face, even if it does smell somewhat stale. I don't want to think about our ship sinking."

"Speaking of sinking," Anderson said, "we just entered city limits. You two need to dive down deeper in the seat if you don't want our local social media paparazzi taking more pictures. I'll try to motor through town as slow as I can, for the sake of your sea sickness. Then we'll get you safely to your lifeboat." The officer lowered her speed as she cruised along.

Great, now the policewoman was getting into the act. He thought about trying to change the subject, but hesitated. He was actually enjoying holding Amber. He snuggled in closer.

She sighed. "I don't want to lose my 'Jack Dawson' to the sea, but we're fighting against our pasts and the danger that lies in our future."

Amber's comment sent a chill down his back. He hoped it was only the overworked air conditioner but understood all too well what she meant. They bumped over a lift in the pavement and heard the sound of a garage door rumbling open. Officer Anderson paused and then drove forward. Darkness surrounded them as she cut the engine and the garage door closed.

"Time to jump ship, people." The locks of the doors popped open and they untangled themselves.

Graham grabbed Amber's hand before she exited and gave it one more squeeze. "We will get through this."

An interior door to the house opened. "Welcome to my humble abode." They followed Michelle Anderson into her home and waited in a cozy living room while she looked for something they could wear. She came back moments later carrying a few sets of clothing for each of them from her and her husband's closet. "Give these a try. We look about the same size."

Graham entered a guest room and tried on the clothing. The golf shirt and cargo pants were not his usual style, which was good. He wondered what their hostess had chosen for Amber. When he re-entered the living room, he was surprised to see her sporting a lacy top and shorts that looked like a skirt. Her feminine look both scared and intrigued him. Her beauty seemed enhanced by a dusting of makeup, but he still liked her natural features best.

She sat in a chair where Michelle worked Amber's hair into a fancy braid. The scent of hairspray filled his nose. His sister had tried to use spray on his hair once. He'd felt as if he had plastic hair like her Ken doll. That was his first and last experience with the product, though his ex-fiancée tried to change his looks several times by buying him expensive hair gels.

The sound of a vehicle pulling into the driveway sent him to the front window where he pulled back the curtain. A woman in khakis and a polo shirt hopped down from a hard top crossover with four-wheel drive. A blue sedan pulled in behind her. She climbed in beside a man wearing a similar outfit. Graham dropped the curtain. "Our transportation is here. Thank you, ma'am, for the loan of your clothing and for your service to this community."

"No problem about the clothes, I'm glad to serve where I can. This will give me an excuse to go shopping. I hope you complete your case without too much trouble." After spraying one more cloud of hairspray into Amber's hair, the policewoman handed them each a shopping bag with the other sets of clothing. She shook Graham's hand and gave Amber a hug as she opened her front door. "It looks like the coast is clear. Let me know how things turn out for you two." Her grin implied she referred to their relationship more than the case. Graham chose to ignore the look the two women exchanged.

He hurried to the 4x4 and found keys and cash sitting on the driver's seat. Amber climbed in next to Graham, finding her own set of keys and a thinner envelope of cash. That should make her happy. He'd learned Amber liked having choices.

Graham shifted the crossover into reverse and backed out of the Andersons' driveway. "You don't think you ever heard of Clint Roberts before?"

"No. I hope our troublemakers haven't heard of him either. So where are we going to find this fellow?" Amber adjusted her air vents and inhaled.

"We're headed for the rolling hills of Tennessee."

Chapter Eighteen

An hour later, Amber surveyed an open field dotted with cattle. Graham parked the 4x4 across the road from a rutted drive. A mailbox with the name Roberts painted in flowing script identified the homeowners. The culvert at the beginning of the gravel path showed signs of caving in, so they opted to walk after parking on a nearby wide shoulder. As they hiked closer, a man stepped from behind an older vehicle.

"Stop right there, you two." Amber stared at the man standing in front of a rusty 1960s muscle car. He had his hands wrapped tightly around a rifle, held in a firing position. The barrel pointed straight at Graham. "Raise your hands, Mister. We don't want any of your bodyguard tricks."

"Look, sir, whatever you heard isn't right. I'm not a bodyguard. I'm FBI if you want to know the truth." Graham held his arms out but didn't lift them high.

"I heard you might be making up some kind of fake story. We wondered if you two might be coming this way looking for me too. Are you all right, Miss Amber? The internet said this guy was holding you hostage because you knew Max Whitney. I figured he must be after your gift from Max and wondered when he'd come after the money I got from old man Whitney."

Amber stepped between the two men. The man holding the rifle lowered it as a concerned look spread across his face. Graham huffed behind her. She held her hands high so Mr. Roberts could see them. "I am fine, Clint. Graham has taken good care of me since the day I met him. He really is from the FBI. You can check his credentials. Someone is after us and they loaded social media with misinformation. I don't know anything about the money you got from Max. That's not why we are here."

"Let me see those credentials, and no funny business." He raised the gun again and waited. Graham handed his badge to Amber, so she could take it to the wary man. She held the badge where he could see it. "Great name for an agent. Guess this proves there's a lot you can't believe on social media. My name's Clint Roberts, but you already know that." He lowered the gun to his side and stared at Graham.

"Yes, sir, we do know your name. There are a few things you can help clear up for us." Graham returned his wallet to his pocket. Amber's shoulders lowered. She hadn't realized how tight she'd held them.

Clint clicked on the rifle's safety and placed it on a towel where his tools lay spread out to one side of the open hood of the car. He wiped grease from his fingers and stuck out his hand toward Amber. Tentatively, she reached for his hand. His grasp was firm, his expression friendly. The man's face was familiar, way too familiar.

"You said you received a gift from Max Whitney?"

His pleasant expression shifted into a frown. "Yes, ma'am. I figured the money was too good to be true. I guess y'all came to take it back. I didn't spend the money. I reckon that was smart of me."

"Whatever you have is yours. If Max gave you something, then you should consider yourself blessed. He took from people more often than he gave until recently. What I'd really like to know is how you knew him." Amber dreaded the answer.

"I didn't know him at all. Last year my wife bought ancestor tests for the whole family as a Christmas gift. His DNA showed up as—" His gaze seemed to be evaluating her looks in the same way she observed him earlier. He cleared his throat. "The test suggested he was my father. I guess that makes us kin."

Amber swallowed as the reality of his words sank in. "I'm his child. I just discovered my, uh, our half-sister. I look forward to getting to know Jade better, once we get her away from kidnappers." Amber forced a smile to her lips. The man seemed nice enough. Her father was the loser. What had he done? Clint Roberts was several years older than her. Had Dad been unfaithful to Mom or possessed no morals before they met? Either way, her insides were quivering in disgust over her father's ethics.

"I was in the foster system for years. I never had a permanent family." His gaze searched her face again as a tentative smile crossed his lips. "It's nice to meet some real family. Would you and your boyfriend, I mean agent, like to come in for some sweet tea?" His smile seemed genuine.

Graham stepped next to Amber. "I hate to break up this little family reunion, but there is something we need from you."

"So this isn't a social call?" Clint's eyes narrowed.

"Besides the money, did Max happen to send you a piece of jewelry with a white stone in the setting?" Graham asked.

"Sure did, my girls love it. One of them probably wore the necklace to school this morning. The rest of my family will be back soon. You aren't gonna take it away from them, are you? The girls seem pretty attached to the bauble. It didn't look expensive, so I figured my ladies could wear the necklace wherever."

"We just need to see the piece for a few minutes and check something. Then your girls can have it back." Amber interrupted the growing tension between the men.

"Good. Like I said, they're real taken with the necklace. My wife is picking the girls up from school on her way back from clerking at the grocery. They'll show you the jewelry." He checked his watch. "I need to be at the factory for second shift right soon after they get here."

Amber looked down the long driveway. "Would you mind if I walked for a little bit? I need to clear my mind. Maybe you guys can talk about that muscle car for a while."

"Help yourself, honey. My girls like taking walks too." He gazed into her face one more time. "I reckon you kind of favor my older gal quite a bit. Finding out we are kin must be hard to take in."

Nodding, Amber fought the sorrow and anger that were punching it out in her stomach. She turned away from the men and headed for the long driveway to wear off some frustration. On her third lap, an orange cat with a twitching tail started following her. She halted her progress, and the tabby wove its way around her ankles. She slowly put a hand under the cat's soft belly and lifted it into her arms.

"You sure are a sweet kitty." Tension ebbed off of her shoulders as the feline started to purr. "Your owner Clint is lucky he never knew Dad. He might have named him Flint or Jasper since Dad gave his daughters the names Jade and Amber." The cat nudged her chin. She laughed at her wandering thoughts.

A compact blue sedan pulled into the drive with a woman driver and two pre-teens inside. Each of the girls looked to be within a few years of Jade's age. They stared at Amber with mouths open as their car passed her and the cat. The sedan halted where the two men leaned against the muscle car, sipping tea. The car doors flew open. An excited conversation took place that Amber couldn't hear. Shortly after, the two girls hustled down the drive.

"I can't believe Allegro let you pick her up. She doesn't like strangers." With the exception of straight red hair, the child speaking could have been Jade's sister. The other girl bore a resemblance to Amber's younger self. She swallowed the urge to cry.

"Hi, girls, I'm Amber."

"Yeah, we know. We're the ones that spotted you on social media. Dad says we got tricked by the internet. Sorry, Miss Amber. I'm Dannie and this is my little sister Kellie."

"I'm almost as big as you." Kellie elbowed her sibling.

"Daddy said you need to borrow the necklace Max gave us. We think it is real pretty." The older girl touched the white stone dangling from around her neck.

"Thank you, I made the necklace myself. My father Max picked out the stones."

The two girls glanced at each other and then focused on Amber.

"Can we call you Aunt Amber?" Dannie's question stabbed at her heart. The sweet faces looking her way made her want to wrap them in her arms.

"Yes." Amber set the cat on the ground and offered her elbows to her nieces. They strolled back up the driveway together. They stepped to the side as Clint drove past them. He hollered out, "Nice to meet you, Miss Amber. I'll see you in the morning, girls."

"Bye, Daddy," the girls shouted, and waved their dad off to his factory job.

"So what do you need the necklace for?" Dannie asked.

"It has a secret compartment. Your granddad Max liked to play tricks on people. He hid a clue in the necklace that will help my friend Graham solve a very important mystery."

"Cool, I like mysteries." Kellie's eyes danced with fun.

"I'd like to know more about making jewelry." Dannie sounded much more serious than her sister. "I draw pretty necklaces hanging from the necks of the female characters I sketch. Do you know how to draw?"

"I do. Drawing is an important part of making jewelry. I call that part the design. Most of my jewelry is one of a kind, because I try to make it very artistic. I even teach college art."

"Maybe you could teach us how to draw better." Kellie looked up with a sad puppy dog expression. Amber's heart warmed toward the girls. Dannie's smile confirmed her interest.

"Perhaps I will, once we solve this mystery. Let's sit down somewhere and see what secret we find hidden in your necklace." The two girls led her into their kitchen and watched her work with the lapidary tools. Amber tightened her hair clip, lifting curls from her neck and face as she worked in the non-air conditioned room. The girls' mother joined them and offered Amber an accepting smile. Once Amber extracted the diode, she prepared to put the piece back together.

"Wait, can we put something in the hidden compartment?" The younger girl ran from the room and came back a few moments later with a broken charm bracelet. "We used to share this, like we've been sharing the necklace. This bracelet's broken, but there's a little kitty charm that might fit in the necklace. It would make us think of you."

Their sweet acceptance washed over Amber like a cool summer breeze. She looked at the tiny charm and cut it free from the bracelet. "I'll make the kitty fit, just for you sweet ladies." They fist-bumped and leaned in closer to watch her work. After extracting the charm, she pieced their broken charm bracelet back together.

Once the task was completed, her own multi-stone bracelet rattled against the table. She released it from her wrist and set it next to the repaired bracelet. "Now each of you will have a bracelet to wear."

"What do you girls need to say?" Their mother put a hand on her hip. The girls wrapped Amber in hugs and a "thank you." The woman offered Amber a glass of sweet tea and introduced herself as Abby while she offered a plate of cookies. "I hope you'll come again."

"I would like to keep in contact with your family." Savory sweetness filled Amber's mouth from the cinnamon-topped snicker doodles. "These are great. I hope you'll share your recipe."

"I'd be glad to share." Abby wrote out the directions while the girls put several cookies into a bag. The girls walked outside to take the treats to Graham while chattering about the bracelets.

Amber slipped the instructions in her pocket and gave Abby a quick hug. "You take care of yourselves. Hopefully the bad guys won't follow us here. We think we lost them once we finished visiting all the obvious relatives." Amber didn't mention the trail of ex-wives. The sweet woman didn't need to be exposed to all of her father's dealings unless it became necessary.

~~~~~

Graham turned from rubbing steel wool across a spot of rust on the old muscle car when he heard the screen door slam behind the running girls. He'd enjoyed talking to Clint. The half-hour he'd spent alone working on several rusty spots gave him time to do some thinking, since he opted to stay outside after Clint left in his wife's sedan.

It felt good to have some space, but his pulse sped up when Amber exited the house behind the girls and headed his way. A few curls had worked their way loose from her pulled-back hair, making her even more appealing. He set the piece of steel wool down on Clint's tool towel and walked toward the beautiful woman. He reached for her hand and swallowed. The temptation to kiss her was strong.

Instead of feeling her hand in his, a lumpy plastic bag filled his grasp. "I hope you like my mama's cookies." Kellie bounced at his side.

The aroma of cinnamon made its way into his nose.

"Maybe Miss Amber can make them for you sometime, if you like cookies." Dannie's shy smile crossed her face as he looked away from Amber's glowing face and nodded to the girls.

"Bye, y'all come again." Abby's voice rang from the porch where the orange cat circled her ankles.

He waved as he and Amber walked back to the crossover vehicle. "I hope we haven't brought them any trouble."

"I do too, but apparently Abby Roberts knows how to use her husband's rifle. She whispered to me when I walked out the door, that she'd run off a few troublemakers in her time. She even goes hunting during deer season to help with their meat supply."

"That's good to know. I noticed Clint take the firearm inside before
~~~~~

he left for work." Graham put the vehicle in gear and headed down the road.

They traveled in silence for a while.

"Are there any more hidden relatives that we're going to meet on this trip? I'm somewhat overwhelmed right now with new family." Amber looked lost in her thoughts as she stared at the passing countryside.

"I don't think our next stop will be directly related to you. Her last name is Roberts. Since your father was making up for his past mistakes, I wonder if the woman we're going to see now could be Clint's mother."

"What a tangled ball of yarn my father made of his life." Amber's tears and crossed arms warned Graham to back off. He tapped on the steering wheel, deciding silence was the best course of action. After a short silence, a weight lifted from his shoulders when deep breathing and soft snores came from her side of the vehicle.

An hour later, he pulled into an urban neighborhood near the Tennessee-Georgia line. Homes built into a hill slanted down toward the potholed street. Most of the houses were small duplexes with two sets of residents sharing one roof. Only the space of a single driveway existed between each unit. It took a while to find an empty parking spot on the car-choked street. Some of the houses looked cared for, but older in years. Other buildings had boards covering windows or showed signs of disrepair and graffiti. People sat on their porches chatting. Children played on steps or on the overgrown sidewalk.

"Wake up, Amber, we're here."

She stretched and looked around. "I'm awake. I've just been doing a lot of thinking with my eyes closed."

"I can only imagine. Let's get this visit over with so we can head down to the best state, Georgia."

"This doesn't look like the type of neighborhood you'd find Dad in."

"No, but it is where someone he hurt managed to make a place for themselves." He exited the car and stepped around a rotten-smelling grocery bag. Several young men whistled from a porch when he held Amber's door open. Her hand drew into a fist, like she was ready to take them on.

"Ignore them. We need to take care of our business and get out of here." Graham led her from the 4x4 and walked several doors down until they reached the side of a duplex with a bright blue door and a pot of pansies sitting on the porch. "This is the place." Graham lifted a lion faced knocker. A pleasant voice called out, asking who they were.

"We're friends of Max Whitney, Miss Roberts. We'd like to talk to you for a few minutes about something he sent you recently." The rattle of locks unlatching came through the door before it opened and the woman beckoned them inside. A well-worn, but comfortable-looking sofa and chair filled her tiny living room. A Bible sat on a coffee table in front of the couch. A few books with library labels sat on a shelf near the door. Other than those items, the room was bare.

"Please have a seat." She locked the door and motioned them to the couch.

"Thank you, Miss Roberts." Graham welcomed the woman's friendly manner.

"Call me Maggie. I was quite surprised when I received a gift from Max, the man who changed my life forever."

"He had a negative effect on just about everyone he knew." Amber's voice reflected bitterness.

"It sounds like he hurt you, too, honey, but I learned the hard way to make my own way in this world." She tapped on the Bible. "God got me through the worst of my troubles. Now I try to do my best to help others. So how can I help you?"

Graham leaned forward. "We'd like to see the piece of jewelry Max sent you. It will only take a few minutes for Amber to remove an item from it that may straighten out one of the man's mistakes. He was trying to right some of his wrongs before he passed away."

Miss Roberts smiled. "I know. When he sent the jewelry, he gave me quite a generous gift to help with my work here in town." She left the room and came back quickly with a necklace. "I've been debating selling the piece and using the money for a good cause, but one of my girls told me I wouldn't get much out of it and should just keep it as a reminder of where I've been."

"So you have some daughters?" Graham asked.

"Only in my heart. I help run a women's shelter a few blocks from here."

"Did you ever have a son?" Amber clasped her hands together.

Maggie paused, her eyebrows raised. "Did Max tell you? I never thought he would admit to knowing me until his gift came. After we stopped dating, he started hanging out with his college buddies and totally ignored me."

"What happened after that?" Graham asked.

"When I found out I was having Max's child, my parents disowned me. So did Max. I was in college and on my way to becoming a success in the world's view. Without any support, I dropped my classes and took a job until the baby was born. For a while, I barely supported my son and myself by living off my savings.

"I put my boy in foster care when we were evicted from our apartment, and wandering the streets. Afterwards I was so lost. I kept making one bad choice after another. One day, I walked into the mission connected to the shelter I now work for. By the time God straightened out my life, I figured Clint was better off where child services placed him. I didn't try to interfere in his life again. There are days when I wonder what happened to him."

"If you had the opportunity, would you like to know more about your son?" Graham hoped the woman would be open to meeting the man he respected, after only knowing him a short time.

"I believe I would. But I don't want to make his life any worse if he holds resentment toward me." Maggie focused on the floor.

"You'll be glad to know we met him and he's a good man. The only downside would be no one adopted him. Clint continued in foster care until he became independent." Graham watched the woman place a hand on her chest.

"I'm sorry to hear he stayed in foster care. Maybe someday he will forgive Max and me for what we put him through." She handed the necklace to Amber. "Maybe he deserves this more than I do."

Amber laughed. Graham had missed her laughter. "I don't think he would have much use for it, but your granddaughters might enjoy having it."

"I have grandchildren?" Maggie Roberts sank back into her chair.

"Yes, you do. I'm sure they would be glad to meet you. Maybe, once Graham and I solve this mystery Max gave us, we can take you there someday, or at least I can. They're my nieces." The two women hugged as the tears flowed.

Graham turned away and stepped into Maggie's small kitchen when his phone rang. When he returned, they were still embracing.

He cleared his throat, interrupting their hugs. "Speaking of the mystery, Amber, please open the stone and retrieve what we need." His voice sounded sharp in his own ears.

Amber looked up and frowned, before she pulled out her tools and dug out another diode. She put it in her pouch with the others and thanked the woman for her help. Amber left the envelope of cash the FBI agents provided for her on the coffee table with instructions to use it for the women's shelter. The two ladies hugged once more while he waited by the door.

Miss Roberts followed them to her porch and waved as they walked away.

"What was wrong with you back there? You were sure a grumpy old man for the last part of our visit." Amber started to walk ahead of him and then slowed.

"Some complications have developed with Jade's situation." His pulse took a leap when he noticed the group of young men they'd walked past before leaning against the 4x4. Their whistles turned into lewd remarks about the pretty lady.

"You don't want to do this, guys." His warning came too late as one of them stepped behind Amber and wrapped his arms around her. Before the aggressor knew what happened, she had him on the ground with her knee on his back. Graham pulled his wallet and flipped it open to his badge. "I'm with the FBI. I suggest you back off and leave us alone or I'll be escorting you to jail."

"And I'll be letting your women know how you act when they're not around." Maggie Roberts had followed them down the street and stood glaring at the guys with fire in her eyes. "These two are part of my family, be on your way."

"Sorry, Miss Maggie." One at a time, the guys held their open palms out to their sides and backed away. The fellow on the ground groaned and crawled to the edge of a nearby porch before pushing to his feet and following his friends.

"You think about what I said, Marcus." Maggie shook her head and watched the young man slink away with his head down.

"Thank you again." Graham shook the older woman's hand.

"We'll be in touch. You take care of your girls." Amber hugged Miss Roberts one more time before they climbed into the vehicle.

Graham checked his mirrors and headed for Georgia. It seemed like everywhere they went, trouble followed from one source or another.

Chapter Nineteen

Amber breathed a sigh of relief as they cleared the urban streets and headed south for Georgia. Graham reached across the console with an open hand. She hugged her arms close and pretended to focus on rows of corn and beans growing in red soil. Her Dad left Maggie Roberts in a mess and only sought to make a difference in the last few months of his life. How could any man be that cruel?

The younger men who attempted to do them harm on the city streets in front of Maggie's home were as bad as her father, just in a more physical way. At least they respected Maggie, who tried to make a difference in their neighborhood. But that woman had deserted her child, just like the succession of stepmothers had forsaken Jade. This world didn't need more troubled relationships. Graham was plenty handsome, but as an undercover agent, would he be around to protect a wife or a family? She wondered if they could develop a relationship from the chaos they were going through.

Who was she fooling, thinking she'd even know how to date someone? As a workaholic she had focused on school and career for all of her adult life. No one had expressed an interest in going out with her, but neither had she been open to the idea. She should tell Graham to forget about possibly getting to know each other better, but couldn't force her mouth to say the words out loud. As Graham turned down yet another country road, she decided to pursue something relevant to their search for the diodes.

"Are we headed to our Georgia Sunday school teacher's home next?"

"Yes." His clipped answer told her he probably had some issues with their relationship as well.

"I know you said you had a photographic memory, but it must be something to remember how to get around on all these off-the-beaten-path roads."

"Not a problem. I grew up in this neck of the woods." His southern twang seemed more pronounced than when their journey started.

"So where exactly are we headed?"

"Rome."

"Very funny."

"I'm surprised you don't recognize the name of the town. Berry is where your father got his undergrad degree."

"So we are picking berries in the center of Italy in northern Georgia, at a college I never heard about, looking for a Sunday school teacher with a crazy last name?" Amber wondered if what she said made any sense. She was getting a little cranky.

Graham looked her way for a split-second and shook his head as he turned back to driving. "Your father never told you about working his way through Berry College? They have a lot of work-study programs for low-income students."

"All he ever mentioned was Ohio State University, where he met Mom. I assumed he did his undergrad studies there too." Another one of her father's lies. He probably didn't want anyone to know about receiving help from the small college. She should ask Mom if she'd ever heard this part of her father's deception. She vaguely remembered something about Dad earning a full ride for grad school. The thought never occurred that he needed any funding for his education.

"A Christian woman started Berry College. Martha Berry encouraged church involvement for all the students when she led the school. One of your father's older professors still believed in those ideals and convinced your dad to go to church. Max got involved in Mary Belle Crackenbush's Sunday school class after the professor pushed him to attend. Your dad told me he participated in her Bible study in order to win the old professor's favor. Some of Mary Belle's instructions from long ago must have sunk in, causing him to begin seeing the error of his ways during the last months of his life."

"So, Dad used Mary Belle for his own benefit. What a jerk."

"But God chose to put words in her mouth, which would eventually have a positive impact on Max. He became a changed person in the last few weeks I knew him."

"It sounds like you are on Dad's side now. He broke my trust too many times." Amber resisted the urge to pout.

"Look, I hate what he did in the past, but for your own sake, you need to think about forgiving the man. In the end, it appears he wanted to set things right through turning in the names of the cybercriminals. He started going to church and getting his heart in the right place. I just wish he'd revealed the names of his fellow criminals sooner." Graham's fingers tapped on the steering wheel for a moment. "Dwelling on his harmful past will only hurt your own mental health and harm those around you. You've got a bigger family to think about than you did a week ago, thanks to this scavenger hunt he sent us on."

Amber felt a headache coming on. She reached over and turned up the fan. "I don't know what to think right now. If you don't mind, I'd rather not talk about anything for a while." Her thoughts tumbled over each other, but she didn't feel like sharing any of them with Graham. She'd made it on her own without much help from family or friends. She could do it again when this adventure was over.

As much as she condemned her father, possibly seeing her new family members again sparked a yearning in her soul. She just didn't know where she'd find the time to visit them with her new business set to get off the ground. Her dad had been a workaholic. She inherited the same drive, which would most likely prevent her from finding time to see either her new or old family.

She'd easily frozen Graham out in the last few minutes, both literally with the roaring air conditioner and figuratively by refusing the offer of his hand and their abruptly ended conversation. Would her heart grow so cold that no family would want to claim her?

A little while later, she reached over and turned down the air. "Sorry."

"No worries. We'll keep to the business at hand." His short answer spoke volumes.

Several minutes later, Amber noticed Graham peering from side to side. He seemed to be searching for something as he increased their speed. She turned the car's fan back to high, trying not to think about her motion sickness as the 4x4 raced down a twisted road. She focused on her new family instead.

"I'm planning on meeting Clint's family again when this is all over. They need to connect with his sweet mother, Maggie. Dad wasn't much of a family man to Mom and me, but he left a legacy of relatives for me. At first, the idea of Clint's family and Jade being relatives was a shock. Once Jade is rescued, a relationship with all of them is something I want to explore." Determination spread across her thoughts. Despite being busy, she wouldn't repeat her father's mistakes. Making time for family needed to be a priority.

"Clint and Maggie seem like nice people. I don't think you will go wrong by getting to know all of them better. During our brief conversation, he talked about putting most of Max's gift into savings for the girls to attend the local community college." Graham gripped the steering wheel and checked his side mirror.

"I'm glad to hear he's making a wise choice." Worry wormed its way into her mind. "I only hope Jade will survive her kidnapping and can get to know Clint's girls."

"About that, I took a phone call from Landon right before you took the diode out of Maggie's jewelry. A woman named Joy showed up at a hospital dehydrated, with a broken arm, and covered in bruises. Someone left her to die. They tied her up in a shed near a remote lake. God must have been watching over her. The property owners came for a fishing trip the next day. They heard her moaning." Graham sped up a little, taking the curves faster.

Amber held on to her belly, hoping he'd get the hint that she wasn't handling the swerving ride. "Is she Jade's nanny, Joy?"

"Yes. The woman told the local law enforcement about overhearing her captors making threats to harm her if Jade didn't cooperate with them. I'm not sure if her injuries indicate your sister didn't cooperate, or if she did, the crooks left Joy on her own when they were through with her." When they entered a straight stretch, Graham drove faster.

Amber groaned. Her stomach and thoughts of her father were tearing her apart. "I hope Jade is able to stay strong."

"Based on what I'm seeing in the rearview mirror, I think they forced information from her. She must have eavesdropped on our conversation about our destinations. Though I can't understand how they keep finding our exact locations. It looks like our friends in the sedan are closing in fast."

Amber's seatbelt tightened across her chest as the other vehicle tapped their bumper. Her stomach rolled. Graham swerved and then regained control. As she looked in the rearview mirror, she saw a gun appear outside the other vehicle's passenger window. *Watch over us, Lord.*

After they sped up and rounded another bend, Graham turned onto a muddy road heading between two pastures. The only thing distinguishing it from a path was the numbered county road sign. They curved down an incline and splashed through a stream crossing, a narrow band of underwater pavement barely visible beneath their tires. A sign marking it as a dangerous crossing made Amber's teeth chatter. The vehicle bounced up a rutted hill. Amber held her hand over her mouth as she looked back at the sedan. The pursuing vehicle slid to one side as it crossed the creek. One of its wheels went deep into the water, stranding their followers halfway off the cement crossing.

"Stop." Amber placed her hand on the door handle, ready to jump out.

"Not a good idea."

Amber started heaving.

He stopped.

The men left their car and started running. She opened her door and leaned toward the ground. Moments later, they sped away as bullets fell far behind them.

Chapter Twenty

"How did you know to take that road?" Amber felt lightheaded, but thankful for their escape.

"I told you, I'm from around here," Graham snapped.

Amber crossed her arms and watched the scenery pass.

They rode in silence until Graham pulled into a shaded drive leading them onto the Berry campus.

"Why are we going to the college?" Amber admired the well-manicured lawns and rock buildings.

"As I mentioned earlier, Mary Belle Crackenbush passed away recently. One of the college professors is handling her estate. I don't have his home address, but according to additional information shared with me during that last phone call, he is teaching a summer class that releases soon. We've got time to take a look at the campus and then catch the man when he finishes lecturing." Graham left the car and headed up a sidewalk leading toward a cluster of rock-covered buildings.

When they walked from between two of the structures, they passed a fountain splattering a welcoming sound. A few steps later, she spotted a long pool reflecting the azure blue of the sky and mirrored images of the rock edifices surrounding them. The peaceful setting melted some of the anger she'd held in. She noticed a student sitting on the opposite side of the pool and sank into a similar position for herself. She ran her fingers across the still waters as God placed His words about still waters in her mind.

Lord, I've been walking through a rough valley in the last few days. Help me find Your peace. Thank You for this moment of quiet.

She stretched out on the rocky edge of the pool and soaked in the sun and God's love. She needed to forgive Dad and try to forget his trespasses. She'd tried to make that exact effort to let it all go before they started their journey but hadn't been successful with all the reminders they'd encountered in the last few days. Too bad she'd never been on this campus before. It looked like a great place to learn. She straightened when Graham plunked down beside her.

She couldn't keep a welcoming smile from spreading across her face. His expression matched hers. "The campus is beautiful."

"It's a pretty cool place to get an education." Graham leaned against her side.

"Did you go here?" Happiness washed over Amber.

"No, my brother did. I went to Georgia Highlands for a criminal justice degree." He shaded his face as a bird flew overhead.

"Does he live nearby?" Amber watched Graham scoop a palm full of water.

Graham shook his head. "We both decided to go to Atlanta to seek our fortunes. We had an apartment together for a while." He frowned and let the handful of water from the reflecting pool dribble through his fingers. "I transferred north when my ex dumped me for my brother." He shook the excess water from his hand and stood. "We need to head for the classroom in the building to our right. It's almost time for class to end." He offered her a hand up and she took it. When he released her hand after she stood, a sense of loss filled her.

~~~~~

The reminder about Graham's ex-fiancée shadowed his mind like a cloud. That romance had come and gone like water over the waterwheel standing next to an old mill on this campus. He needed to remember Amber was nothing like the other woman. He could see the vast difference now.

He blew out a mind-cleansing breath and held the classroom building door open for Amber and his future. Once they entered the interior hallway, a flow of students exited the classroom where the professor could be seen talking to some lingering scholars. Graham sensed Amber at his side and cautiously slid his hand around hers.

When the last student exited, he released Amber's fingers and entered the classroom to meet the man whom he presumed to be Mary Belle's executor for her estate. The slightly stooped gentleman had a head of wavy-white hair and wore a pair of horn-rimmed reading glasses.

"Professor Albertson?"

"That's me. What can I help you two with?" The professor peered over the top of his half-framed spectacles.

"We need to talk to you about the estate of Mary Belle Crackenbush."

"Bless her dear heart. I miss that woman something fierce. I hated to see her go to her reward, but I'm pretty sure she made it to the good place. If you knew her at all, you know what I mean." He shuffled a stack of papers together and tucked them into a shoulder bag. "Walk with me to Barnwell Chapel. I'm meeting a couple of students there for a moment of prayer, but we can talk until they arrive."

Graham walked next to the professor as the older man expounded on the virtues of Mary Belle. Amber followed silently behind them, seemingly listening or lost in her thoughts. He needed to concentrate on finding out if the professor knew anything about the gift Max had sent Miss Crackenbush. He opened his mouth to ask his question, but the
~~~~~

professor turned at the door to the chapel and asked how they knew the woman.

"As a Sunday school teacher, she influenced a man called Max Whitney. Amber is his daughter. I'm from the FBI." He briefly flipped open his wallet long enough for the badge to show. "We know Max sent Mary Belle a piece of jewelry with a white stone in the design. He hid something important to an ongoing case. I'm trying to break up a crime ring using an object hidden inside the jewelry. As her executor, we were wondering if you saw something like it in her effects."

The professor waved them into the log-sided chapel as he scratched his chin. Wooden beams arched overhead, supporting the dark planked ceiling. Their footsteps echoed as they crossed the ancient hardwood floor and sat on a stiff pew.

"I vaguely remember her mentioning the man when she got the pin from him. She wore it to church for several Sundays after she received the piece. Mary Belle added his name to the prayer list and made a generous donation to the choir fund in his name not long afterward. As far as its location, you'd have to take that up with the company I hired to sell her things. The auction happened yesterday, so they might remember who bought the piece. I think they keep records, but I haven't been over to settle with them yet." He gave Graham the name and address of the company.

As Graham thanked the man, he noticed Amber's bowed head. He prayed she was getting things sorted out with God.

The door behind them creaked open and two students entered. The professor's lips turned up, creasing into a pleasant display of wisdom's wrinkles.

"I hope you find what you need. Mary Belle always told her students to look for answers above and not below." He pointed toward heaven. As Graham and Amber stood to leave, the professor ushered the waiting students into his pew. A memory of Max saying something about looking up fluttered across his memory. Maybe the words were a coincidence, but he'd keep them in mind in case they held value. He nodded to the professor as he and Amber left from the other end of the seat, exiting the building in silence.

As they walked back to their car, Graham let the whisper of the breeze through the trees along the path wash over his soul. The old professor had given him a good reminder. He needed to trust God to work things out for them. Only one more stop remained after seeing the estate sales company and then hopefully they'd have all the clues needed to solve this case. Maybe Amber wasn't in God's plan for him at the moment, but he'd learned to trust her and prayed one day they might become more than friends. He recently realized he did have the capacity to trust a woman of her caliber with his heart.

His shoulders relaxed as they drove into the town and parked on Broad Street in Rome. Amber asked to wait in the 4x4. Since they parked right outside of the business' plate glass window, he figured she would be safe. When he entered Davidson's Realty and Estate Sales, an old high school friend sat behind the welcome desk. He hadn't seen Kyle Davidson since moving to Atlanta, but the guy recognized him. They wrapped each other in a rib-crushing bear hug, left over from high school football days.

"What brings you to town, Graham? I haven't seen you since you took off to work for the FBI."

"I'm actually working on a case you can help solve for me. I heard you handled the estate sale for Mary Belle Crackenbush yesterday."

"Sure did, she was a sweet old lady. Folks loved her up at the college and our church. I can't think of anything she owned worthy of an investigation."

"A man I had under scrutiny sent her a pin made with a white stone. I don't suppose you recall something with that description?"

"I do recall the white stone because of a strange incident. Mary Belle didn't have much jewelry. We put the ten or so pieces she had in a box for the auction. Some of her church lady friends started the bid because of sentimental attachments. Then this woman came in, dragging a scared-looking girl, and outbid them by hundreds of dollars. When she paid for the bid, she grabbed the pin out of the box and threw the rest back on the table. The girl started to say something to me, but the woman told her to 'shut up or else.' I made sure the church ladies got what they should have had in the first place and didn't charge them a thing."

"Good for you. I'm sorry we didn't get here in time, but you may have given us some information about a kidnapping situation related to the case. Did you see what kind of vehicle they were driving or details about what they looked like?"

"I didn't see their car. They must have parked around the block from Mary Belle's house. The woman and the kid both had blonde curly hair. The woman was tall but that's about all I know. She took a bidding number but wouldn't leave a name or address."

"The description of the girl sounds like the one we are missing. There's been a BOLO out on a girl named Jade Whitney, but you might have missed it."

"Yeah, I've been too busy with the estate sale to hear anything newsworthy. I hope my description will help."

"Thanks, Kyle. I owe you a steak dinner next time I'm in town."

"I hope I don't have to wait too long."

Graham shook his friend's hand, failing to commit about when he'd be back. He'd send his friend a steakhouse gift card to make sure he kept his word. When Mom and Dad retired to Florida a few years back, his ties with Rome had ended. He took one last look at the town as nostalgia washed over him. Despite the circumstances, he'd enjoyed visiting the old stomping grounds. He needed to figure out who the woman was with Jade and where they took the missing pin.

Boom. A shot rang out. Amber's scream pierced the air as the window of his friend's business shattered.

Chapter Twenty-One

Graham scrambled on all fours toward the exit. Kyle crawled in behind him, a pistol in hand. "I've got your back, buddy."

"Thanks, man." As Graham reached for the doorknob, another bullet burst through the upper part of the door, leaving it hanging on the bottom hinges. Pulling up into a crouch, he grabbed a magazine and tossed it across the room to draw fire away from the doorway. Shots followed the object through the air, sounding closer than before. Graham rushed from the door and released the safety on his gun. He couldn't return fire. The 4x4 and Amber blocked the shooter and the man trying to drag her from the front seat.

The shooter aimed high above the vehicle. It looked like the man wanted Amber alive. Graham seemed to be expendable. He stepped closer to the vehicle as he saw Kyle signal he'd go around the back of the building. Taking a hint from his opponent, he also fired high and toward the city square, which had suddenly cleared of people.

The sound of a smaller caliber gun split the air. The shooter on the other side screamed in pain as he fired another round. His shot went wild. Amber grabbed her upper arm and grimaced.

The man fell back into the back seat of his car, holding his own arm. "We need to get out of here. Push her in the back seat with me. You're going to have to drive. They got my right leg."

The next scream came from Amber as she ground out a "hi-yah." Her would-be captor groaned and headed toward his companion with a bloody nose.

Graham pointed his weapon at the man trying to reach the car. "Stop right there. Neither of you is going anywhere." Sirens sounded. The shooter laid his gun down. Good, someone had called 911. Graham hoped the locals could identify who the bad guys were.

Kyle waved to the policeman. "Those two men shot up my business and were trying to kidnap this woman. Thanks to my old high school buddy, Graham, they aren't going anywhere." He went on to explain his role in the take-down.

When an ambulance pulled up, Graham insisted that they check Amber's arm. Amber flinched when the medic rubbed the grazed flesh with an antiseptic.

He looked down at the gauze and stared. "I'm sorry ma'am. It looks like whatever you had implanted in your skin just fell out."

Amber gasped. "I didn't know I had anything there, other than my arm has been hurting ever since I had my first run-in with those people."

Graham stepped closer with an evidence bag in hand. "Let me have that. We need to send it off to a lab, but I have a feeling this is why we've been so easy to follow."

By the time they filed police reports and the local authorities agreed to send the implant off for evaluation, Graham discovered the two arrested men had records for taking money to do criminal acts. They'd confessed to receiving a hefty sum from an unknown woman to kidnap Amber and bring her to Gorge Bluff, Alabama. A sinking feeling filled his chest, knowing the ringleaders were a step ahead in the game. He thanked the officers and Kyle before climbing into the 4x4. Amber slumped in the passenger seat as they headed out of town.

His mind wandered to Jade and the missing diode as he drove down a four-lane road toward Max's hometown in Alabama. A sense of urgency helped in making the decision to head for Gorge Bluff using the most direct route on the interstate. He phoned Landon and let him know about their latest incident and the information Kyle Davidson shared about spotting Jade. His teammate decided to reverse their wild goose chase back to where he'd picked up the regional agent. Landon would drop the woman at her station and start on a path for Gorge Bluff.

Graham's gut rolled as his thoughts focused on their adversaries, who now included a woman being way ahead of them with Jade in their clutches. Amber gripped the armrest between them and sat up straight in her seat. She'd been pretty upset when she heard the news about Jade at Mary Belle's auction. She needed a distraction or she was going to have a meltdown, or start spouting inane one-liners. He'd prefer the latter. Her humor was better than the present silent treatment.

"What can you tell me about your great-uncle Jethro?"

Her chest heaved from a blown-out breath. "He wasn't too much older than Dad. Granny called him her oops brother, but the age difference made it possible for him to help my grandmother as she grew older. Great-Uncle Jethro's hardware store seemed like a treasure shop when I explored it as a kid. I was around ten the last time I saw him, other than at Granny's funeral. By the time of her death, Dad wasn't talking to anyone down here. We swooped in for the funeral and left as soon as it was over, never to return again. I guess that will change today."

Amber started chatting about her childhood. Graham welcomed the distraction as they drove closer to Gorge Bluff. He pulled down the visor, blocking the lowering sun's rays. A few stray clouds reflected the light, creating streaks of color. Amber stopped talking and sighed as she looked at the sunset.

"It's beautiful." Graham admired the colorful heavens.

"God knows how to color the sky. It makes me want to get out my paints." The sun highlighted a glow on Amber's cheeks.

"I thought you were only into jewelry." Graham watched her smile as he momentarily took his gaze from the road.

"I studied all the art media and performed well in most of them. I still occasionally dabble in something besides the lapidary arts."

"I'm glad you're lapping up all the arts." Graham decided to try being funny.

"Hey, I'm the one that should be spouting crummy comedy." Her giggle proved she enjoyed his attempted humor.

"At least I've got you talking again." Graham adjusted his visor.

"Yeah, sorry about that." The last color of the day faded and darkness filled the car. "Do you think we're going to make it before Uncle Jethro goes to bed?"

"Probably not. I'm debating about whether we forge ahead for Jade's sake or call it a night. I'm fighting to stay awake."

"As I recall, my great-uncle lived on a farm out in the country. It might be hard to locate his place late at night. GPS may not even exist on dirt roads. Jethro taught me how to shoot. He might decide to take a shot in the dark."

"Ah, our comedienne is back." Graham pulled into a hotel parking lot. He booked two adjoining rooms while Amber waited, hunched over in the car with his sidearm. He prayed he hadn't made a mistake by delaying their travels but knew they both needed to rest after their long day.

~~~~~

Graham tossed and turned, finally managing to get a fair amount of sleep before dawn. He didn't hear anything from the adjoining room, so he headed down to the lobby and picked up a couple of muffins, juice, and coffee. He stopped to grab a paper and sat outside his room on an ancient metal lawn chair, watching the sun come up over the horizon. Minutes later he returned to his room, flipped through the paper, and was relieved to see an article retracting their BOLO. He picked up the tray of breakfast items and tapped on the shared doorway.

When Amber opened the portal, smelling of hotel soap and shampoo, his heart did a handspring. He fought the urge to touch her damp ringlets. It was a good thing his hands carried the muffins and drinks. He swallowed. Graham's mouth felt like cotton as he held the food out toward her.

"I see you've been busy. Thanks for getting something for breakfast. I am totally starved." Her smile made his day.

Graham found his tongue as he forced his emotional reaction to back
~~~~~

off to a low simmer. "You clean up well." Boy, that sounded dumb. He stuffed a muffin in his mouth before he said anything else. Waving, he closed the door behind him. He needed to hit the shower himself.

Once he'd cleaned up, he knocked on the door again.

Amber opened it with her bag of clothes in hand. "I'm ready when you are."

Graham grabbed his own belongings and dialed the office to let the manager know they were checking out. A loud conversation outside the hotel room made him pause and look through the peephole before opening the door. Two men, who could easily pass as the first ones who'd tried to abduct Amber in their sedan strolled past, still in pajama pants and tee shirts. As their loud discussion filtered through the door, Graham heard the words, "boss lady" and "Gorge Bluff." Amber grabbed his arm and squeezed it until pain filled his muscles.

"Should we try to confront them?" Her voice trembled.

"I don't see anyone else with them. They would have known we were here and attacked if we hadn't taken that implant out of your arm yesterday. It looks like they're going to eat breakfast and will need time to get dressed before they leave. I think the best thing for us is to quietly get out of here and head to your great-uncle Jethro's as fast as we can." He cracked the door open and they hustled into their vehicle. He pulled the visor to the side of his face as they passed the hotel office. Amber leaned back and hid from view at the same time. Once they were on the road, Graham relaxed and set the cruise control for five miles above the posted limit. He didn't need to draw any unwanted attention by getting a speeding ticket.

Amber kept checking her side mirror. He did the same but saw no evidence of anyone following them. They didn't have too far to go before reaching Gorge Bluff. After cruising down Fayette Avenue, the main drag through town, they parked in front of Jethro's Hardware. The lights were on and a few early morning customers entered the door ahead of them. A gray-haired gentleman in overalls stood at the cash register, laughing with a customer.

"Does that look like your great-uncle?"

"I think so, he's a lot older than I remember, but he resembles Dad. Let's go ahead and talk to him before those two men show up to give him trouble."

An overhead fan swooshed above their heads as they opened the door to the store. The smell of wood, metal, and a hint of fertilizer saturated the air. Bins filled with everything from gloves to nails lined narrow aisles. A chime announced their entrance, and the older man turned their way.

"Amber girl, is that you?" A smile creased his face until he spotted

Graham standing behind her. The older man whipped a rifle from beneath his counter and pointed it toward Graham's chest. "Who you got with you, sweetie pie?"

"Graham is one of the good guys, Uncle Jethro. I told you about him when we called the other day. He's with the FBI and has been protecting me. Save your shooting skills for the criminals that may come after us. They're the ones who convinced everyone Graham kidnapped me."

"The TV news folks did say it was phony, but I wasn't sure who to believe." He lowered his gun and offered Graham a firm handshake. A waiting customer wanted a handshake, too, so he could brag about meeting a real FBI guy. Graham obliged.

"Could we talk to you in private for a few moments?" Graham needed to hurry things along before people started asking for his autograph.

"Sure, Milton sometimes minds the counter for me. I'll turn the business over to him for a bit while you tell me what's been going on. I'll take a hug from my dear Amber." He wrapped his arm around his great-niece and led them to a back room. They sat around a table as Amber told him about their travels.

Jethro leaned back in his chair and frowned. "That no-good nephew of mine came through here a while back. Max made some changes to your grandma's tombstone. I didn't like what he did, but he didn't want me switching it back. I figure since he's dead I can put my oldest sister's stone back to rights. I reckon you better check it out before you leave town."

"I will definitely visit Granny's grave. I'm sorry I haven't been here for a while." Amber reached out and covered her great-uncle's hand as tears flowed down her cheeks.

Graham cleared his throat. They needed to get the diode and move on to the graveyard to find out if Max left a clue there. "Did your nephew send you a piece of jewelry made with a white stone?"

"Max sent me something specially made by Amber. I've been wearing it ever since I got the little thing." He pulled the string tie from around his neck and released the stone slider holding it together. "Your dad said he'd like me to hang on to the slider and I promised I would, since I knew the artist. He said you made this tie clip and I should be proud to wear it."

Amber pulled out her tools and released the diode from its hidden compartment.

"I haven't seen one of those in years." Jethro scooted closer and squinted at the piece. "Max and his daddy used to have a bunch of these lying around the house when your father was a boy."

Graham tapped Amber on the shoulder. She gathered her tools and put the diode in with the others. "I hope we can come by later, but right now we better head to the cemetery and see if Max left us a clue there, since you said he did something to your sister's gravestone."

"Max was an interesting child. He always wanted to see if he could fool the other kids by giving them something to solve. I hope you can find a solution soon and will stop by later."

~~~~~

Amber knelt in front of Granny's tombstone and ran her fingers along the large bronze nameplate. The setting for her granny's information seemed out of place. Next to the plate, the etching of Grandpa's name and dates reflecting his life and death broke the granite surface of the marble marker. She looked closer and noticed tiny screws holding the bronze marker in place. "Does your knife have a screwdriver inside?"

Graham leaned closer and offered the knife. She carefully unscrewed the plate, revealing the rest of her grandmother's name properly etched in granite. The back of the bronze plate revealed a circuit board with ports for twelve diodes. "I think we just found the motherboard."

"Good. Let's get out of here before some bad guys or gals show up and try to put it all together."

"Too late for that, Graham Jones, or should I address you as Agent Crusher?" A woman dressed in a black power suit stepped into their view. Diamonds twinkled from her neck and ears. Blonde curls framed her angular face. Two men stood by her side. One of the men had his arms wrapped around a squirming Jade. His blonde curly hair bore the same color and texture as Jade's and the woman's.

A glimmer of recognition flashed across Amber's memory. When she'd been fighting with the man at the art studio and the rest stop, she'd noticed the attacker had curly blonde hair. Now, she realized how closely it matched Jade's. Both men had similar height and build as the ones who'd been pursuing them in the beat-up sedan.

"Amber, meet Mrs. Whitney-Stanley, Jade's birth mother and chairwoman of the board of MAX Enterprises." Graham's voice held recognition as he looked between the two women.

A ripple of shock hit Amber in the middle as she looked up at the woman who had impacted her life as a teen. Her father's ex-wife glared down at Amber from her perfectly powdered nose. Her face should have been one of beauty, but the hate behind the woman's heavily lined eyelids made the younger woman cringe.

"How did you find us?" Graham asked.

The woman's face gleamed with distaste. "When my daughter Jade thought Nanny Joy was going to die, it didn't take much to convince her to spill her guts about what she heard when you thought she was sleeping. Her information was very helpful since you obviously found our tracker sometime yesterday."

"Who told you we were at the graveyard?" Amber felt anger boiling
~~~~~

as she looked at the woman.

The woman put a hand on a hip and batted her lashes. "Milton back at the hardware store told us you'd gone to the cemetery. He was pretty easy to sweet talk."

"But how did you know to come to Alabama? I don't recall telling Jade about coming here." Graham frowned at the woman.

"Big ears here heard you two talking about Mary Belle Crackenbush and your final stop at Gorge Bluff when you thought she was asleep. The brat mentioned you were collecting some cheap jewelry."

"I'm sorry, Mr. Graham. They were going to kill Nanny Joy. I had to tell them about the stones." Jade squirmed in her captor's arms.

Amber held her breath for a beat. It didn't sound like Jade had given away the hidden diodes.

"Shut up, little sister." The blonde man sneered.

"I don't want to be your sister." She popped her head back into his chin.

"Sorry, our mother's blood flows through both of us." The blonde-haired man tightened his grip on Jade.

"Yeah, but she didn't raise me. Joy did. My nanny took the time to show she cared." Jade stomped on her brother's foot. He groaned and tightened his hold.

"Stop your squabbling, children." Mrs. Whitney-Stanley held out an oversized purse. "I'll take what you have in your hand and everything else you've found during your travels. You could have saved all of us a lot of trouble if you'd just cooperated back in your quaint little art shop and let us find what you've been looking for."

"We don't have all the answers you're looking for yet. The only clues we've collected are a bunch of stones." Graham's gaze met Amber's and then he looked down at the loose gravel covering the ground underneath her hands. The gravel in the Alabama soil had prevented grass from completely covering the surface where her grandmother's remains lay deep underground. Granny had always been a tough woman, just like her granddaughter. Amber clasped a handful of the loose stones in one hand. She leaned the motherboard against the tombstone, placing the bronze plate over it, which sent wrinkles across Mrs. Whitney-Stanley's flawless face. Amber still fisted Graham's knife in her other hand and waited for him to give a signal.

"This won't be your problem, Graham, if you make her turn everything over." Mrs. Victoria Whitney-Stanley fluttered her mascara-laden lashes at the agent.

He nodded. "Amber, give her the stones. Now."

Chapter Twenty-Two

Graham watched Amber throw the handful of pebbles and sandy earth toward the heads of the criminals facing them, then spring to her feet. He used their confusion to wrestle one of the men to the ground and place handcuffs on the man's wrists.

Jade ducked her head while the rocks rained down. The young girl lifted one leg and kicked back at her brother's knee. He howled in pain. She stepped away and pushed her mother to the ground.

Amber circled the man who once held Jade. He held up one hand in surrender as he sat on the ground and swiped grit from his eyes. His blonde hair stood in spiky curls covered in pebbles and sandy red soil.

As Mrs. Whitney-Stanley stood back up, Graham stepped over to hold her in place. The woman twisted in his arms but couldn't find release.

The other criminal who lay cuffed nearby spoke up. "Sorry, boss lady, we tried to catch 'em before they found out about you and—"

"Shut up, doofus." Victoria Whitney-Stanley kicked out at her henchman, and he rolled to his side in pain. She glared at her captors. "You may have captured me for now, but you still don't have a clue about the information you are trying to find or the names of my cohorts who will come to stop you next."

The threat hit home. What she said was true. Until they figured out what to do with the diodes, there would be no end to the fear hanging over them. The pictures he'd seen of Martin the mole didn't resemble the men in cuffs. Could there be others out there, besides the man who kidnapped Jade?

~~~~~

A few hours later, Amber once again sat at the table in Great-Uncle Jethro's storage room. Jade sat quietly nearby with her arms hugging her body, looking defeated, despite reassurances that what happened wasn't her fault. Amber removed the diode from the last stone. Graham had located Mary Belle's missing pin in Victoria's possessions when the police officers collected personal items from Mrs. Whitney-Stanley.

"Did your father ever do anything with the stones or diodes that might give us a clue as to what his hints mean?" Graham asked.

"Not that I can remember. He was more into explaining how quartz had important uses in his business. He did teach me how to make a quartz radio once. We had to climb the hill behind Granny's house before we
~~~~~

could hear any broadcasting." A fleeting memory crossed Amber's mind. There was a connection. She needed to figure out what she was missing.

They spread the diodes out across the tabletop. Each had a color painted on its side. The motherboard they'd found hidden behind Granny's tombstone nameplate held no clues as to the placement of the twelve pieces, or what purpose they served.

"Didn't you say something about the twelve tribes being represented by stones on a breastplate?" Amber stared at the array of diodes.

"I didn't think that was the verse. Max only mentioned the engraved name verse in Revelation." Graham crossed his arms.

She pulled up a search about stones in the Bible on her phone. Amber filtered through Old Testament references until she found the description of the breastplate." I'm going to arrange them in the biblical order by color and see what happens. The only problem would be that there are several with very similar colors."

"I guess it is worth a shot." Graham leaned closer as Amber worked. His breath warmed the back of her neck as she attempted to focus on the work at hand.

She looked at the list of stones and read through them in her head. Sardius, topaz, carbuncle, emerald, sapphire, diamond, ligure, agate, amethyst, beryl, onyx, and jasper. "I'll give it my best try."

She started the process and soon discovered that each diode featured slightly different width spaces for their prongs. Dad had made sure the details worked for each to fit into its own slot. The board filled up quickly. But the mystery remained about what to do with the completed unit. She held the panel up in the air and observed it from all angles. The letters engraved along the side of each diode caught her eye. They spelled, M-O-U-N-T-S-A-R-A-R-A-T.

Memories of taking a homemade quartz radio up the mountain as a child blazed across her mind. At that time, Granny had shared the story of Noah with her. She'd misheard what Granny called the mountain where the ark settled. Amber called it Mount Sara Rat, thinking Noah named the place after her childhood friend, Sarah, and a rodent. She and Dad had coiled wire around a paper tube, connected a diode and an earphone into the device, and listened to a radio station. The results amazed her then and still did.

"I know what we need to do." Amber pumped a fist in the air. "Jade, did Dad ever make a radio with you?"

She shrugged. "He showed me a homemade one once. I was more interested in downloading music on my device."

"Do you still have your earbuds?" Amber's excitement grew as the possible solution came together.

"Yeah. It's all I have left of my phone since you guys threw my cell out the window." She pulled the plugs and wires from her pocket and offered them to Amber.

"I need a few things from Uncle Jethro's hardware store and then we've got a mountain to climb." Amber started her search for the items she needed.

"What's this I hear about you three taking out the enemy?" Landon walked into the room and joined them as they talked about climbing the mountain. "Sorry I missed out on catching the criminals in action."

"We've caught three of them. None of them were Martin. I still haven't heard anything about his whereabouts. I sent a message to the boss, but he didn't reply." Graham followed Amber as she loaded her arms with items needed to create the radio.

"I tried calling him. It went to voice mail. I guess he's busy catching up with his old acquaintance, Miss Winifred Grimsley." Landon winked after insinuating their boss might be romancing the art teacher.

Amber laughed, knowing there was more between the couple than she had a right to share.

Graham nodded. "That could be the case. Right now, Amber is going to make a radio using the diodes and motherboard we found as part of the setup. Then we'll head up the mountain to see if it works."

Jethro helped Amber locate a roll of copper wire and a cardboard cylinder. "I reckon this will work for what you want. Just watch out for the ants."

"Let me guess, do you have a shotgun-carrying Aunt Ruby or Aunt Opal?" Landon laughed at his joke.

Amber grinned at his question. "Ha-ha. Now who is being a comedian under pressure? There are a lot of fire ant hills here in Alabama."

"They're also in Georgia, Landon. Their sting is worse than a wasp. Some people have bad reactions, so be careful," Graham added.

Amber nodded. "I had a bad reaction when I was a kid. So did Dad. I guess an allergy to fire ants must run in the family." She wound the copper wire around the tube and attached it to the motherboard, along with Jade's earbuds, using a hot soldering gun from the hardware store's equipment.

Great-Uncle Jethro made his way down an aisle and came back with a green bottle of bug spray. "You might need this for the other pests like chiggers and ticks."

"Thanks, I'd almost forgotten about those tormentors." Amber gratefully added the bottle to their supplies.

"I know about ticks, but not chiggers. What does a chigger look like?" Landon picked up the bottle and ran his finger down the list of strong ingredients.

"You'll never see one and if you use the spray you won't have to endure a torturous week or two of them burrowing under your skin." Amber shuddered, remembering past experiences with chiggers.

"Amber thinks we'll be able to finally figure out what Max wanted to share, if her hunch is correct about him wanting us to make a radio. We'll be looking up, just like Max and Mary Belle Crackenbush said we should. Do you want to hike up a mountain with us?" Graham asked.

"I'd love to, once I put on some of the bug spray." Landon sprayed on a heavy dose after watching Amber and Graham do the same application.

~~~~~

Jade agreed to stay with Uncle Jethro. The girl planned to call Mama Julia and help Jethro mind the store while the others drove to the base of a mountain not far from Gorge Bluff. Amber noticed a car slow down when they parked their car, but the driver, wearing a dark hat and sunglasses, continued on down the road without turning in. She was getting paranoid about someone following them and was glad when the driver kept going.

Amber led Graham and Landon as they hiked up a barely used trail. Tall grass brushed against their legs. She prayed the bug spray protected their skin. When they neared the top, the tree growth grew sparser and shorter. The sun burned down on their backs. Amber pointed to piles of red soil spread across the warm landscape.

"Those are the fire ant hills you need to avoid, Landon."

When they reached the summit of the mountain, Amber set up the crystal radio and waved her hand for everyone to be quiet. She pushed the earbuds in place and listened. A faint sound filled her ear. At first, she wasn't sure what she heard. She pointed the radio in different directions until she clearly recognized her father's voice reading off names, addresses and other contact information. She handed one of the buds to Graham. He pumped his hand in the air and kissed her cheek.

"Hey, Landon, I need your cell phone to record what I'm hearing. I don't think my sat phone has that function."

Landon switched phones with his fellow agent as Graham and Amber continued to listen. "I hope we can get a good recording and save it for the courts before Martin shows up to interfere." He pushed the record button and held it close to his earpiece.

Landon waved his baseball hat in front of his face. "I'm going to get out of the heat for a bit. There are a few shade trees over there."

"Take your time. I want to make sure we get all of this, just do us all a favor and keep watching and listening for someone trying to sneak up on us." Graham turned back to recording.

Amber watched Landon walk away and then concentrated on watching Graham.

When the loop finished and Graham had recorded all the
~~~~~

information, he tried to send the recording into cyberspace. "Ugh, I've got no bars, no service, no sending the information until we get back to civilization."

"At least we have the information Dad hinted about." Between Graham's peck on her cheek and solving the mystery, Amber raised her hands in victory and started to circle around until Graham held up a hand, halting her movement.

"I'll take that phone and the radio." A man who matched the pictures she'd seen of Jade's abductor stood on the trail they'd climbed. His dark hat and sunglasses resembled the ones of the driver who had slowed down earlier. Amber's suspicions had become reality. He pointed a handgun at them.

"You must be Martin." Amber glared at the man.

Martin's panting was heavy as he frowned.

"How did you find us?" Graham raised up into a squat.

"I watched you take down Mrs. Whitney-Stanley. After that I just followed you and waited." He gulped the air and waved his gun again.

Amber's breathing had been short when they'd first reached the top of the mountain. Since she and Graham stayed in one place for the recording, their respiration had returned to normal. That might be an advantage, except for the gun pointing at Graham. She looked around, expecting to see Landon nearby.

"If you're looking for the other agent, I knocked him out cold while you two were occupied." He waved the gun over his shoulder toward a lump on the ground under the small grove of trees. Amber heard a *thunk*. Graham had dropped his phone and now used Martin's half-turned body as an opportunity to rush forward. She picked up the phone and stepped out of their way as they wrestled on the ground. The gun fired.

Amber's breath caught. A harsh laugh sounded as Martin pushed Graham's writhing body away. Without thinking, she ran to Graham and knelt beside him. Blood poured from his side as his face turned pale and he passed out. Her anger erupted. Martin grabbed her from behind and lifted her away from Graham's limp body.

"Now you're going to show me how to disable this primitive radio and get rid of whatever tower is transmitting what you heard."

"The name of the Lord is my strong tower." The words from Proverbs filled her heart and her tongue as she offered up a silent prayer. *Heavenly Father, give me strength like I've never had before. Thanks for having Dad give me self-defense lessons.*

"Where is that tower?" He jerked her closer to his body, lifting her into the air. As he dropped her back to the ground, he provided the momentum she needed to throw him over her head and into a hill of ants. The gun he'd tucked into his belt flipped away before he landed. She picked it up and pointed it at him as the ants began to swarm.

"If you move one inch, I'm taking out one of your limbs."

The man screamed as the ants started biting. "Please, can I get off this ant hill?"

Amber nodded, keeping her distance as he rolled to the side and started beating off the insects. She heard a sound behind her and hoped it wasn't another bad guy. "Landon?"

"Yeah, I'm here, with a pounding headache and a twisted ankle. I've got a pair of zip ties we can put on this guy until reinforcements get here." He limped past her. "I was able to get a call through on the sat phone. Help should show up soon. I told them we needed an air ambulance." He put the restraints around Martin's hands and feet. The man's skin had begun to swell around the welts. Amber laid down the gun and rushed to Graham's side. His chest lifted with irregular breathing. He moaned in pain.

"Please, Lord, don't let him die. I don't want to lose him." She felt his hand briefly tighten around hers as she prayed aloud. "Hang in there, my special friend." She brushed her lips across his hand and heard him sigh.

Landon stripped off his shirt and started applying pressure. "He's a tough piece of jerky."

"Ow, you're the jerk." Graham moaned and passed out again.

They stayed by Graham's side until the helicopter landed and took him and the welt-covered criminal away. Landon limped down the mountain with Amber leading the way back to the 4x4 vehicle.

She called over her shoulder, "Are you sorry you didn't take the helicopter to the hospital?"

"Graham wouldn't have wanted you walking alone. My only regret is making you go slow because of me. You probably want to run to the hospital to be with your guy." His voice sounded like a cross between teasing and genuine concern. Amber prayed for Graham's life instead of reacting to his comment. Deep down, she hoped one day he would be her guy.

~~~~~

She spent the next two days with Great-Uncle Jethro and his wife, Lottie. Amber shared about her newly discovered siblings with her relatives and promised to come for a visit at least once a year. She renewed acquaintances with Jethro and Lottie's daughter, Elsie and her children.

It felt good to connect with family, but she needed to head home and see if she could salvage her credibility as a business owner. Before it was time to meet Landon for her ride to the airport, she asked Jethro to drop her off at the hospital for one last visit with Graham. Sedation had kept him groggy the last few days when she stopped by to pray at his bedside. She hoped he would remember today's farewell.
~~~~~

Waves blipped across the monitors by his bed. It was good to see he would make it, but she hated the pallor of his face, a face that had been so full of life until two days ago. She reached for his hand and held it to her lips. "Goodbye, sweet friend and protector. I'm going to miss you. We're both carrying baggage we need to work through. Maybe one day—"

A mischievous smile spread across his lips. "How about today?"

"What?" Amber felt his warm hand wrap tighter around hers.

"How about today we start dating? That way we can work through this together and then—" The smile turned hopeful and spread across his battered face.

"I've never dated before. Work and my relationship with Dad always got in the way." Maybe it was time to make a change. Exploring a closer relationship with Graham could open the door to new, happier possibilities.

"Would you be willing to make time for me? We can go slowly until we know each other better." Graham pulled her hand to his lips and looked at her with a pleading expression.

A rush of yearning made Amber's heart flutter. "Yes, I'd love getting to know you better. I believe I might have a crush on you, Agent Crusher." She leaned in closer and brushed her lips across his. It felt like coming home.

Epilogue

The following spring, blossoms once again dotted the trees as Amber walked across campus for the last time as an instructor. Her retail studio had taken off like a jet after the grand opening almost a year ago. She no longer needed to supplement her income by teaching part-time at the college. Making the national news added to the fame of her business rather than hurting it. She'd hired Kara as the afternoon and weekend manager. Together they'd employed additional clerks to help run the place.

Jade and Mama Julia were regular customers for classes and art supplies. Amber took time to do some online lessons with the Roberts girls. Every Friday night belonged to dates with Graham. He'd kept his promise to keep their relationship slow and simple as they grew closer. Their bond grew into one with hints of a sweet future. His unwanted fame on the internet led to a desk job as the public face for the local FBI office since his boss retired. Amber didn't mind the change one bit. They both pledged to keep work from interfering with their growing romance. His new position and her added employees gave them time with each other.

She hurried to her store and set up for a new ring-making class. Kara hadn't given her a roster yet, which surprised Amber. Her manager was usually more efficient. Amber laid out paper and pencils for the students after Kara assured her the class boasted a full group of students. Tonight's class would involve designing a ring and choosing materials.

The front door bells jingled as people entered and chatted inside the store's retail space, which often happened before a class. The chats always made the group more enjoyable when the participants bonded into a family.

Amber moved out into the hallway to welcome her students. Jade and Mama Julia walked in first with smiles on their faces. Several of her friends from college followed them, including Loretta, who'd forgiven Graham for denting her car. The older woman's friends, Honey and Annabelle, bustled in behind Loretta with hints of pink blush adorning their wrinkled cheeks.

Scott, who was doing well as the Arts Department Chair, his wife Ginny, and their children came in next. Their adopted daughter, Melissa pushed baby Treasure Hope in an antique stroller. Amber bent closer to take the hand of the toddler, who bounced in her rolling seat.

Ginny stood nearby with her hands resting on a timid-looking boy's shoulders. "This is our new son, Mason. We're happy he joined the Hallmark family last week."

Amber knelt in front of Mason. "Do you like art? You can sit with your family at this special table."

He nodded but turned to Ginny for confirmation before following Amber to a front table.

"Hello, Magpie." Miss Freddie and Kent Russell entered the room after Scott and Ginny's family found their places.

She'd heard the older couple had endured an adventure of their own, playing an important role in tracking down the rest of the cybercriminals. They'd been under a gag order until the recent court case was resolved, so Amber had plenty of unanswered questions about their adventure. She knew they'd been seeing each other since then and was thrilled for the older couple.

Her thoughts were interrupted when Graham and the whole Roberts family walked in, followed by Aunt Lottie and Uncle Jethro. She gave everyone hugs as they entered. What was going on?

"Hi, dear." Mom and Howard hugged her as they joined the class.

"I'm happy and a little confused by seeing all of you tonight. Is there something that I should know about?" Amber searched her mother's expression for a clue until someone bumped her side.

"We just want to learn how to make a ring, that's all." Jade's goofy look said otherwise, but Amber decided to play along.

"All right, students, the first step is to design your ring. Here are several examples of drawings I've done for your inspiration."

Graham stuck up his hand. "Which one do you like the best, teacher?"

Amber felt heat flow up through her cheeks. Why was he acting like he barely knew her? One of the designs featured braided gold and she'd actually thought it might be a nice design for a wedding band. She held the paper high so all could see it. Everyone oohed and aahed.

"Could you show us how to make that design?" This time it was Great-Aunt Lottie who spoke up. She was usually a quiet woman, but she seemed giddy tonight.

Graham stepped closer. "Please make it in your favorite color of gold." Amber started to have a hint of what might be going on. Hope entered her heart. When Graham handed her a box with raw pieces of gold laid out for her use, suspicion turned into reality.

She set aside the materials she'd planned to use for the demonstration. Then she carefully tapped his strands of white gold into the braided ring. She suspected the ring should be in her size, based on the smiling faces around the room. When it was finished, she held it up for inspection. Graham slipped it from her fingers and knelt at her side as a hush filled the room.

"Amber, I love you with all of my heart. Will you marry me?"

"Yes." Her heart pounded in her chest as he stood.

Graham's lips met hers. Happiness poured over her soul like a fountain. Amber had his love, a devoted family, and friends who would support her throughout life.

Thank You, Lord, my rock and foundation, for every blessing!

The End

THANK YOU!

Thank you for reading this book from Mt. Zion Ridge Press.

If you enjoyed the experience, learned something, gained a new perspective, or made new friends through story, could you do us a favor and write a review on Goodreads or wherever you bought the book?

Thanks! We and our authors appreciate it.

We invite you to visit our website, MtZionRidgePress.com, and explore other titles in fiction and non-fiction. We always have something coming up that's new and off the beaten path.

And please check out our podcast, **Books on the Ridge,** where we chat with our authors and give them a chance to share what was in their hearts while they wrote their book, as well as fun anecdotes and glimpses into their lives and experiences and the writing process. And we always discuss a very important topic: *Tea!*

You can listen to the podcast on our website or find it at most of the usual places where podcasts are available online. Please subscribe so you don't miss a single episode!

Thanks for reading. We hope to see you again soon!

ABOUT THE AUTHOR

Bettie Boswell has always loved to read and write. That interest helped her create musicals for both church and school and eventually she decided to write and illustrate stories to share with the world. Her writing interests extend from children's to adult and from fiction to non-fiction. In addition to writing novels she has written other works, including leveled readers, magazine articles, and contributions to lesson plan collections, devotionals, and short story anthologies. She is a minister's wife, church musician, has two grown sons, one daughter-in-law and three grandchildren. She loves the arts and shares her doodles, and photography from her daily walks on social media. This is Bettie's first suspense publication. She is looking forward to exploring Kent and Miss Freddie's adventures in the next book.

Dedications and gratitude:
To all those who helped shape this book:

To God, who gave us creativity; Ann Cavera, critique partner; ACFW Scribes critique group 201, Mary Vee, Kathy McKinsey, Dave Arp, and Jen Dodrill; my editor Michelle Levigne; book cover designer and publisher Tamera Kraft. To my husband who patiently waited for his turn at the computer. To two art teachers who long ago had an influence on my interest and ability in art, Miss Grimm and Miss Winnie. And in memory of my parents: Mom, who nurtured a love of books and Daddy, who wrote down family history and tried to teach me a few things about rocks and radios.

https://sites.google.com/view/bettieboswellauthorillustrator/home